"I'm not aski

"You're not asking

"Can the one be enough?" Finn's pulse faltered then revved. She needed this time in Westbend, and who was Finn to steal that from her?

Ivy studied him, contemplative. Pretty. Even prettier now that he'd seen her heart on her sleeve while she'd worked alongside him tonight. "Maybe. I do need the place if I'm going to stay in Westbend with the girls. And the first week of work at the café has been great. It made me feel valuable and alive again. Not that the girls don't do that. They do. But I want them to know the version of their mom who existed ten years ago."

"I'm looking at that woman right now. I don't know where you think she went, but everything you've done since you arrived here matches everything you just said about that old version of yourself."

"Thank you."

"You're welcome." Finn could only pray he wouldn't come to regret passing up the second opportunity he'd had to send Ivy away…

Jill Lynn pens stories filled with humor, faith and happily-ever-afters. She's an ACFW Carol Award–winning author and has a bachelor's degree in communications from Bethel University. An avid fan of thrift stores, summer and coffee, she lives in Colorado with her husband and two children, who make her laugh on a daily basis. Connect with her at jill-lynn.com.

Books by Jill Lynn

Love Inspired

Colorado Grooms

Visit the Author Profile page at Harlequin.com.

Choosing
His Family

Jill Lynn

LOVE INSPIRED
INSPIRATIONAL ROMANCE

LOVE INSPIRED®
INSPIRATIONAL ROMANCE

ISBN-13: 978-1-335-48867-1

Choosing His Family

Copyright © 2021 by Jill Buteyn

This edition published by arrangement with Harlequin Books S.A.

For questions and comments about the quality of this book, please contact us at CustomerService@Harlequin.com.

Love Inspired
22 Adelaide St. West, 40th Floor
Toronto, Ontario M5H 4E3, Canada
www.Harlequin.com

Printed in U.S.A.

Trust in the LORD with all thine heart;
and lean not unto thine own understanding.
In all thy ways acknowledge him,
and he shall direct thy paths.

—*Proverbs* 3:5–6

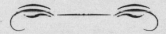

To God be the glory

Chapter One

Spring snow pummeled Finn Brightwood's windshield as his tires turned to ice skates beneath his vehicle, a fitting representation of the predicament he'd somehow gotten himself roped into.

He tapped the brakes, righted the truck and managed to stay in his lane. Thankfully, hardly anyone was out tonight, so there was no vehicle behind him or coming his way. He'd been to Denver despite the weather, because he hadn't believed the report—they were wrong so often. But if anything, tonight's dump of white moisture had amounted to even more than had been expected. With a four-wheel drive vehicle beneath him and years of snow driving experience, he'd be fine. It was the rest of the world he had concerns about.

The trip to Denver had been a necessity he'd happily have avoided, but the local cattlemen's group had decided—without his consent—that as their newest member, he should host their annual dinner. Unfortunately, since he'd purchased the Burke ranch last fall, he more than fit the newbie description. And now, despite having no idea how to host a dinner—or party or whatever they wanted to call it—for thirty people, he was a handful of days away from doing exactly that.

Which explained his trip tonight—he'd needed more supplies than Len's Grocery in the small town of Westbend could provide, though he'd purchased what he could there first.

His headlights brightened the snow lining the ditch and the flash of tire tracks that cut through the growing depth.

Tire tracks? Had he seen that right? There'd been no vehicle to go with the tracks. Maybe the snow had just blown a certain way, creating the illusion…or maybe there was someone who'd gone off the road.

Finn scanned his rearview mirror for approaching traffic. Not spotting any, he slowed to a stop in his lane. He'd never sleep if he didn't check on whether his eyes had deceived him.

Since no one was approaching from behind, he reversed until just after where he'd noticed the break in the snow. Sure enough, tracks cut through the white. And they were filling in quickly with the additional accumulation. Another hour and they likely wouldn't be visible.

He could call for help. But what if whoever it was had already been rescued? He'd investigate first, then decide. Finn parked on the shoulder, donned his Carhartt jacket and grabbed the gloves and hat he kept in his truck console along with his flashlight. He'd worn his wool-lined leather boots tonight, so they'd hold up fine. And his jeans—not exactly snow gear, but they'd do.

He hopped out—the snow spitting at him like a wildcat with icy claws—and strode to the start of the tracks. His first sweep came up empty. He went slower the second time, the beam from his flashlight barely reaching far enough to help him.

There—near a small pack of evergreens, the tail end of a vehicle protruded. Thankfully, this part of the road didn't veer straight into a cliff. He started down the hill, the snow slipping and sliding underneath him.

The SUV must have been crawling when it connected with the trees, because it looked as if the damage to the hood and bumper was minimal.

He approached the driver's door. "Hello—are you okay in there?"

No answer came from the body leaning against the window, but a wail sounded from somewhere inside. Finn eased open the driver's door, which was fortunately unlocked, catching the woman who'd been propped against the window before she tumbled out.

"Ma'am? Are you awake?"

She blinked once, twice, her confusion evident. There was no blood that Finn could find, but the crying multiplied. He peered into the back seat, and then he was the one blinking. Not one, not two, but three little girls filled the row. They were strapped into car seats and, based on the lung power they were packing into those wails, seemed to be relatively uninjured.

"I'll check on your kids." Finn let her door close to keep in the heat. He fumbled for his phone while switching to open the back door. "Hey, girls." He kept his voice even-keeled. "Everything's going to be okay." *As long as your mom isn't injured beyond what I can see.* But she was wearing her seat belt, so she hadn't gone too far from home base. Finn would guess she'd knocked her head against something on the way down the slope.

One of the girls—the one farthest from him—

continued shrieking. The one in the middle stuck two fingers in her mouth. The one closest to the door he'd opened launched into a slew of questions.

"Is Mommy okay? What happened? Why was it so loud? We went—" She made a roller-coaster motion with her hand.

"I know you did." Poor kid. "I'm working on getting you girls and your mama some help, just hang tight. I'm going to shut this door to keep the heat in, but I'll be right outside on the phone, okay?"

Finn closed the door and dialed 911. He explained what he knew of the situation and detailed their location. The operator said help was on the way, though of course the night had produced plenty of accidents and crews were diligently assisting everyone in need.

Directly after he hung up, Finn's phone rang. His sister, Charlie. If he didn't answer, she'd worry. She knew he'd driven to Denver tonight.

Finn gave her a thirty-second snapshot of what he'd stumbled across.

"Do you need anything? Do they? What can I do to help?"

"Nothing. Just stay home. The weather is nuts. Please don't go out in it," he continued before she could protest. "I've got to go. I'll update you later."

He moved back to the front door and opened it again. "How're you doing up here?"

This time the mama hen was alive and well. She clucked over the girls in the back seat, checking for broken bones and signs of blood. He waited for her to assure herself they were fine—or at least close to it.

When she turned back to face him, he continued, "I called for help to get you out. I'm not sure how long it will be before they arrive, so I'm going to climb in the passenger seat and wait with you all. Okay?"

Distrust radiated from her, and while Finn understood it, he certainly wasn't going to leave the four of them alone. So he did what he'd planned to do and added himself to the mix.

Once he shut the passenger door, a hushed warmth replaced the swirling, angry snow.

"How did you find us? The minute we started sliding off the road, I had this flash of fear that no one would ever know we were down here." Her SUV boasted Connecticut plates. The real question was, how in the world had the four of them ended up here?

"I was driving back from Denver and saw your tracks in the snow. Thought I was imagining things at first, but then I decided to double-check."

A crack in her wariness surfaced, and she softened. "Thank you. I can't imagine what would have happened to us if you hadn't."

He wanted to tell her everything would have been okay. That she would have woken up, called someone, gotten help. But the truth was, he didn't know what would have gone down.

Thank You, God, for the nudge that made me turn back.

"I'm Finn."

"Ivy." She wore a knit hat over blond locks that skimmed her shoulders, and her features were petite. She shifted toward the back seat. "These are my girls. Lola, Sage and Reese."

The trio matched their mama in hair color, and at least two of them—Reese and Sage—also shared their mother's distrust. Lola was the one who'd launched into an inquisition when he opened the back door.

"How's everyone doing back there?"

"We went—" Lola made the same motion she had earlier, but with a few more loops and dips involved this time, like a fisherman embellishing the story. That had to be a good sign. Reese continued to whimper, and Sage kept the same two fingers in her mouth like a plug. His gaze slid back to Ivy. "Any injuries?"

"Not that I can tell. Everyone seems intact. Please let it be so." Her eyes welled at that, and Finn felt that familiar sense of compassion—the one that got him into trouble—swamp him.

"It's going to be okay. We're getting help."

"I'm not sure there's enough help in all the world for the mess we're in." She said it under her breath, as if it wasn't meant for him, but he heard it just the same. And it sent warning sirens blaring, because assisting someone on the side of the road was one thing, but Finn couldn't get involved with another damsel in distress.

Not when the last one had absolutely demolished him.

Ivy Darling woke the next morning to faint light gliding through blinds, her mind instantly filling with last night's events—flashing emergency lights, panic over her girls and the unexpected kindness of two strangers.

Two, because not only had Finn stopped to help them, but his sister, Charlie—a redheaded spitfire— had shown up shortly after his arrival. Around the same time as the emergency crews.

Finn had growled at Charlie, *I told you not to come.*

Charlie had chirped back at him, *We both know I don't listen very well.*

Ivy had instantly liked Charlie, and Finn's concern for his sister's well-being had also upped her trust levels for him. Charlie had brought blankets, toys, snacks and drinks for the girls, explaining that she used to foster-parent and had gotten into the habit of keeping supplies at her apartment. She'd been a comfort and a godsend, and when the paramedics had given the triplets the all clear medically but tried to insist that Ivy go to the hospital to get checked out, Charlie had been the one to support Ivy's definite no.

As if she could have left her girls. Charlie had understood. She'd bundled them up and brought them here—to Finn's ranch house. Charlie had insisted on staying with her and the girls throughout the night to make sure everyone was okay.

Ivy moved to a sitting position on the couch she occupied, her body quickly announcing its dissatisfaction with her movement.

Her muscles were like meat that had been tenderized, and her head... She could use a dose of extra-strength ibuprofen. But her girls were alive and well, and nothing else mattered. They were laid out like three-year-old burritos on the floor, with lots of blankets and pillows, and Ivy's Good Samaritan, Charlie, slept on the recliner chair across from her. She'd checked on Ivy numerous times last night and now finally slept.

Ivy could safely say she'd never met anyone like these people. Once she continued on with their journey to her parents' house in California, she probably wouldn't ever again.

Wrapping the blanket around her, Ivy eased off the couch. If she stayed here, she'd wake everyone else with her movements. She wandered from the den toward the kitchen, the smell of coffee overruling her awkwardness at finding herself in a stranger's home.

Thankfully, she'd been able to find something comfortable from her own clothes to wear for sleeping. At her request, Finn had fished out their overnight bags from the Suburban before it had been towed into town.

The man who'd stopped to rescue them sat at the dining room table, some papers along with a mug of coffee in front of him. No lights were on, but the quiet glow of morning was slipping through the windows, a faint blue hue dancing off the fresh snow and illuminating the mountains that surrounded the ranch.

The great room had a stone fireplace that rose to the ceiling and was flanked on both sides by windows. With beams traversing the ceiling and dark leather furniture dotting the space, it was something out of a Western magazine. Ivy wouldn't be surprised to find an antique gun mounted over the front door.

She paused in the doorway, unsure whether Finn knew she was there, whether to enter.

"Coffee's in the pot. Mugs are in the cupboard above."

"Thanks." She followed the best scent in the world and found a white mug. From her quick glimpse around the place, she observed everything was simple with clean lines...even down to the dishes. Definitely not a woman's touch in the house, but it was still tasteful, and Ivy felt strangely comfortable. Probably Charlie had something to do with that. When Ivy had protested staying here last night, Charlie had shut her down quickly.

Where else are you going to go?

A hotel. There has to be one in town.

There's a motel, but then what? You don't have a vehicle. And I'm not sure I trust that you're truly okay.

I'm the one who backed you not going to the hospital tonight. Charlie's gaze had encompassed the girls. *And I understand why. But now you have to give me this. Let me check up on you all tonight and make sure you're okay. Otherwise I'll be panicking that you're having issues while you're alone with the girls.*

That argument had won Ivy over. She might not *want* to need help, but resisting it last night could have been detrimental to the triplets. She couldn't risk her pride causing them harm.

Ivy poured coffee into her cup, steam rising, and lifted it to her nose to inhale. Dark roast, she would guess. God bless Finn.

"My sister left some of her little creamers here. Above the mugs."

Ivy found them and added a small dollop. "God bless Charlie," she murmured before bringing the liquid to her lips. Finn's mouth crinkled slightly as if he was amused by her, and he went from stoic to appealing in a flash.

Should she sit at the table with him? Or cross over to the couch and chairs filling the great room?

She chose the table but went one seat down so that she wasn't directly across from Finn and they weren't forced to make awkward eye contact.

"I don't know how to thank you and your sister for rescuing us last night."

"You don't need to. Besides, we both know she was the one who demanded you all sleep here so she could check on you and the girls, so let's give credit where it's due."

"You were the one who saw our tracks and stopped, so…"

A slight shrug came from the man, but that was the only acknowledgment he gave. A slight shrug and another one of those almost smiles. Ivy strangely wanted to earn a full one.

His expression morphed into a scowl when his attention went back to the notes in front of him.

"I hope it's not my presence making you that upset. I can go, drink my coffee somewhere else and let you be."

"It's not you. I just…" He groaned. "I'm supposed to host the local cattlemen's dinner on Saturday night, and I don't have a clue what I'm doing. That's why I was in Denver last night—grabbing supplies—or I wouldn't have driven past you on my way back to the ranch."

Ivy had exited the freeway hoping to escape the storm and find lodging to wait it out. She'd never imagined any of what had followed. *Thank You, God, for sending Finn and Charlie when You did.*

"My whole life back in Connecticut was hosting dinner parties and schmoozing clients for my husband."

"Was?"

"Yes…my husband passed away. He took his own life after he was caught embezzling from his employer." *Ugh.* Ivy's lids shuttered. "I'm not sure why I shared all of that."

It was like standing on the side of the highway, holding up a Hot Mess sign for all the world to see.

"I'm sorry." Finn let the silence sit, giving his condolence credit. Not filling in with drivel like so many did.

"Thank you."

"You can probably give Doug's body shop a call this morning to check on your vehicle, but with the damage… Charlie thought it may take a week for them to get it back to functioning." Charlie had told Ivy that she was a mechanic. Unfortunately, she didn't run the auto body repair shop. That would have definitely come in handy.

Finn took a sip of black coffee. "It needs new tires if you plan to drive it through any more harsh weather."

Ivy winced. She'd known the tires were on their last leg. Unfortunately, the money she'd grown accustomed to in her marriage was long gone.

"Doug will need your insurance information, too." Finn's eyebrows joined together, as if questioning if she even had insurance.

She did. She wasn't delinquent on everything. "Okay, I'll call him this morning."

A week wasn't bad, but what would they do in the meantime? Ivy would have to find a place for them to stay, which took more from her meager savings. Unless... unless she could work a deal with Finn that would benefit both of them. Last night when Charlie had driven her and the girls from the accident to the ranch, she'd mentioned that Finn's property had a vacation rental on it. Ivy had wondered if that was where they would stay, but then they'd ended up at the house, in the den.

"This might sound a little crazy, but I have an idea."

Finn eased back from the table, his spine ramrod straight. Already distancing himself. Not the best sign.

"I can help you with that." She pointed to his notes. "I could host a dinner with one hand tied behind my back."

His eyes narrowed. In the dark of her vehicle last night Ivy hadn't been able to tell the color well, but this morning, with the additional sunlight now streaming inside, she could tell they were the hue of underripe blueberries. He had blond hair—definitely not as pronounced as his sister's short red locks—and strong, defined cheekbones that would make any woman weep with jealousy. His warm skin tone carried a pink tinge as if he was uncomfortable or embarrassed or wanted to be rid of her.

And yet, she continued anyway. "Your sister mentioned you have a vacation rental on your property. What if I traded you a week of me and the girls staying there in exchange for taking over the planning and hosting for your cattlemen's dinner?" Ivy had never made a suggestion of that magnitude before. Prior to marrying Lee, she'd been confident and carefree. She'd had lots of friends and even more dreams. She'd been invincible. But each year of their marriage, she'd lost a piece of herself. Now she hardly recognized the thirty-two-year-old woman who stared back at her in the mirror every morning. But even broaching the idea gave her a surge of adrenaline—crazy and reaching though it might be.

"The unit is unfinished. The Burkes—the couple I bought the ranch from—were having money troubles, and they thought a secondary form of income would help, so they started renovating the old bunkhouse into a vacation rental. The beds are in and the bathroom is done, but the small kitchen is unfinished."

They could live without a kitchen. If she and the girls ended up at a motel, they wouldn't have one anyway. "That's okay. We don't need much. I don't want to pressure you into this. It would be a huge plus for me because we'd have an affordable, safe place to stay for the week, but don't consider it unless it would be a help to you. I'm not asking for charity. I'm asking for a trade."

Ivy's world might have crumbled in the last year, but she was determined to find a way to redeem things for her girls. Determined to show them everything would be okay. And if that meant weathering a bump in the road that amounted to a week's delay in Westbend, Colorado, so be it.

And if it meant asking Finn Brightwood, a man she

barely knew, for the chance to make that happen…she would ask all day long.

"So—" she sent up a prayer that Finn would at least consider the idea "—what do you think?"

I think I can't get involved.

Finn pushed back from the table under the guise of grabbing more coffee. He refilled his mug, accidentally clanging the lip of the pot against his cup. Hopefully, he hadn't just woken the girls and Charlie. The den connected through the hallway behind the kitchen, but he didn't know whether the French doors were closed or not. His sister had likely checked on everyone throughout the night and now deserved the rest.

You cannot make this deal with this woman, Brightwood. Don't even consider it.

Before purchasing the Burke ranch, Finn had worked on an oil rig in North Dakota. A woman he'd met in town had convinced him that she'd needed to escape an ex-boyfriend. That the man was abusive to her. Finn had spent a lot of time and effort helping her, figuring out how she could protect herself. They'd fallen for each other—or so he'd thought. But after a stint when he'd been working, he'd come back to town to find she'd *married* the guy. Finn wasn't even sure if the stories she'd spun about him being abusive were true. The situation had left him unsure of everything.

He'd vowed that there would be no more rescuing of damsels in distress—real or fake—and now, thanks to his sister, he was right back at square one. And Ivy's story was…wow. Not only had her husband embezzled, he'd then taken his own life, leaving her with *triplets*. How could he have done that to her?

The fact that Ivy was fighting so fiercely for her girls impressed Finn, but that still didn't make any of this his problem.

Only…it was hard to turn off the part of him that cared and rescued. That instinct *was* a problem. He was working on it. And taking this deal with Ivy…it would be backtracking.

Finn couldn't dally anymore without being obvious, so he returned to his seat. Ivy had moved to the window behind the dining room table, watching as the world woke up, the morning glow illuminating her pretty features. Her blond locks were pulled back into a short ponytail. She was small-framed, but *timid* wasn't the right word to describe her. She had spunk. To ask him—a stranger—to make a trade was gutsy. Strong. He respected that. Maybe too much.

The problem was…he wanted what she was offering.

This dinner was a major stress for him. He would have fought hosting it harder, but the cattlemen's group hadn't even entertained another option. They were amused by him being a newbie, and they'd declared him as the host before he'd gotten a word in edgewise.

It wasn't rescuing if he was getting something in return, was it?

"I'll show you the rental, and if you think it's up to snuff even though it's not finished, you're on."

Lord, I think I might be absolutely crazy for doing this. Prove me wrong, would You?

Chapter Two

"Red light." Ivy called the command across Finn's great room from her perch in the kitchen. While she often found it amusing that everyone on every HGTV show demanded an open floor plan, it was turning out to be a godsend. Ivy could manage and wrangle the girls, who were in the living room, while she puttered in the kitchen prepping for tomorrow night.

Lola came to a complete stop with precision.

Reese was next, and she righted her body so that it aligned with her sister's...and so that she didn't get caught for going too far. No one wanted that scenario, because a burst of tears would surely follow any censure.

Sage went another three steps before heeding the change in direction. Both of her sisters called out the infraction with a vengeance.

Ivy wasn't raising demure girls. They loved each other fiercely and lived fiercely, so full of life that she almost never made it until nine thirty before falling into bed each night. And she wouldn't have it any other way.

Every moment since they'd veered off the road she'd

given thanks to God that the accident hadn't been worse. That she and the girls were okay. Ivy was sore, sure, but it wasn't anything some ibuprofen couldn't tackle. And cranky muscles and a slight headache would fade in time. The day after the accident, she'd taken the girls to Dr. Sanderson in Westbend. He'd been incredibly thorough in making sure they were okay and had told her what signs to watch for after the fact. None of the girls had displayed any new symptoms. Yet another thing to be thankful for.

Ivy pulled out the spices for the potatoes. "Sage, honey, you need to go back to the starting line." Which was the stone fireplace that divided the front windows.

Two fingers—upside down—slid into Sage's mouth, and she returned to the start without complaint.

Ivy called out, "Green light," and the game continued.

It was a strange thing indeed to make herself at home in a stranger's kitchen—especially a man's. But Ivy didn't have a choice, and she was fine with the agreement she and Finn had come to. She was even enjoying planning for tomorrow night.

Finn had told her casual was the name of the game. They were ranchers, after all. Ivy had taken that up just a notch. They were still having barbecued beef. The plates were still throwaway, but thankfully, Finn had purchased good-quality ones in Denver. He'd given her a budget and let her borrow his truck to get additional supplies. She'd found affordable cloth napkins, because the thought of paper made her cringe. She'd also managed to include some battery-operated tea lights and small glass jars in her purchases, along with the ingredients to doctor twice-baked potatoes and make her favorite barbecue sauce from scratch. The meal might be casual, but it would be *good* if she had anything to say about it.

The bunkhouse, as Finn referred to it, was a pleasant surprise. Tiny and rustic, it had a small bedroom with just enough space for a bed and dresser and another small bedroom that could only hold bunk beds. The girls had been rotating through the bunks with one sleeping on the floor so that no fights over fairness ensued. Though half the time, by morning they crawled into each other's beds anyway, so Ivy didn't know what the fuss was about.

The minuscule living room held two chairs and a coffee table, and the space for the kitchen cabinets and small appliances gaped like a missing front tooth in a child, with only the capped hookups dotting the wall. Finn should consider finishing that portion. Ivy imagined the bunkhouse could make some nice supplemental income.

Even unfinished, the space had more than upheld Finn's end of the bargain. Which was why Ivy was so determined to make good on hers.

The man definitely didn't have time to host a dinner. What would he have done without her help? She'd barely seen him in the four days since the accident. Their conversations had been short and businesslike, which Ivy was okay with. She wasn't here to become best friends with Finn Brightwood. And she also wasn't planning to stay in Westbend. Everything she was doing was for her girls—which meant that after this they'd continue on to her parents' home. Even if that thought made her stomach ball into a fist of concern. Dad didn't think she'd made the right choice in marrying Lee, and he'd been vocal about it. Made it tough to imagine living with her parents. Ivy was hard enough on herself. She knew she'd made bad decisions. She didn't need assistance heaping on the guilt.

The best thing Lee had given her was the girls, and even that hadn't been easy. When they'd had trouble getting pregnant, Ivy had asked for IVF. Lee had agreed, and she half thought he'd been relieved by the idea of being less involved. He'd been good to the girls when he was around, but he'd never wanted them the way she had. Never craved a baby the way she had. Three babies had been a shock, but Ivy had rallied around the idea quickly. She'd known the girls were meant to be.

"Green light!" She called out the final direction, and Lola and Reese slapped the island, giggling. "Time for a new round. Sage, you're back in."

Their pounding footsteps were interrupted by the front door opening. Finn stepped inside and scanned the space—his house—full of them. Ivy swallowed a sigh begging to escape. She'd been hoping not to bother him.

"Hello," he greeted them with a stoic nod.

"Hi, Mista Finn." Lola tromped in his direction. "We had jelly sandwiches for lunch, and then Mommy made us nap. I saw a kitty by the barn but it ranned away from me."

"Lo, honey, let's give Mr. Finn some space. We're playing a game, remember?"

Lola's brow furrowed with distaste at the redirect.

"It's okay. She's fine."

Lola took Finn's permission and ran with it. "Do you want to play with us, Mista Finn?"

Ivy's lips twitched. Lola's pronunciation of *Mista Finn* made him sound like a rapper or a DJ.

"He doesn't have time to play Red Light, Green Light, Lola. That was nice of you to offer, though." Ivy met Finn's gaze, an apology written in hers.

His eyes crinkled at the corners. "Who says I don't have time for a game of Red Light, Green Light?"

Ivy's cheeks heated. "You really don't have to… We'll be out of here shortly."

Finn's smile sparked, and she forgot what she'd been protesting. "You afraid I'll win?"

"Something like that."

Lola tugged on his shirtsleeve. "I'm not afraid you'll win."

"Then let's play."

The four of them lined up at the start while Ivy rolled napkins around disposable cutlery that Finn had purchased. Thankfully, it was of good quality.

"Green light!" Ivy's call was answered by stampeding contestants, but Finn veered sideways while the girls traveled straight—in the island's direction.

Ivy laughed. "Red light."

Finn stopped with his nose pressed against a front window. Lola launched into an explanation of how the game was *supposed* to go, and Sage removed her fingers from her mouth to assist her sister.

"Mommy, can you pause us?" Lola asked.

"Sure."

She marched over to Finn. "Mista Finn, you gotta go straight." She motioned with her arm. "To the island where Mommy is. That's how you play the game."

"Oh, really? Red Light, Green Light must have changed the rules since I played it last."

Lola took his hand and led Finn back to the fireplace.

"Start us over, Mommy. Mista Finn didn't know how to do it. Come on, Reesie. Come on, Sagie."

Lola forced her sisters back to the starting line despite their complaints, and the game resumed. Finn had *a lot* of trouble reaching the island.

He tripped over the coffee table.

Got the red and green commands confused.

Froze in a funny statue whenever Ivy called red light.

He was, in effect, the best toy the girls had ever played with for five minutes of their young lives.

Ivy hadn't expected to be smitten in any way, shape or form by Finn Brightwood, but today was like meeting the man behind the mask for the first time.

It was a good thing she and the girls were leaving town once her vehicle was fixed, because Ivy wasn't about to make another terrible decision regarding a man. She'd fallen for Lee fast, and she'd ignored every flashing warning sign along the way. Just because Finn could play a game with her girls and entertain them for a couple minutes didn't make him safe on a long-term basis.

She knew quite well that beginning impressions didn't always portray the truth beneath.

"Okay, last round." Finn and the girls gathered by the fireplace again, and Ivy called red light first. No one took the bait, so she continued going back and forth.

On a green light, Finn smacked into the couch—on purpose—and hopped and howled in pain, grabbing his shin, while the girls shrieked and took advantage of his injury. Ivy laughed so hard she couldn't form the words for red light, so the triplets came all the way to the island, celebrating their victory with high fives.

Ivy might need to have a chat with them about compassion. She knew Finn was messing around, but they didn't.

Finn came over to congratulate them on their victory. Reese viewed his approach with caution but didn't burst into tears.

"Are you okay? Did you hurted yourself?" Sage spoke around her fingers.

Finn's grin was of the knee-swirling variety. At least that was how it affected Ivy from her perch behind the island.

"I'm fine. Thank you for checking on me."

"I don't think you were actually hurt." Lola inspected him as if she was a scientist and Finn was her test subject.

Finn winked at her, and Lola snickered. The little know-it-all. She was too confident for her own good.

"Okay, girls, why don't you figure out something else to play for a bit?" Ivy had brought a bag of items over to the house to keep them occupied. The three of them ran to it and began pulling out toys, arguing over what to play.

Finn stayed across the island from her. "So how's the prep going?"

"Great!" *Too much perk. Take it down a notch.* "Good, I think. I'm planning to have barbecued beef and buns, twice-baked potatoes, salad and dessert. I also have a few appetizers to set out."

"Okay." His brow furrowed.

"What? Isn't that what we talked about?"

"Yeah, I just… Will you need help getting everything done on time? I could ask Charlie—"

"You don't need to recruit your sister. I've got this covered."

He didn't look encouraged.

She kept her voice low and calm even though his

doubts hurt a little. "Listen, Finn, I realize that we don't know each other well enough for you to trust me, but you can on this. I'm not going to drop the ball or not have the food or space ready. You've more than held up your end of the bargain letting us use the bunkhouse. I promise—I'll take care of my end."

After a beat, he nodded. "Okay. Sorry to doubt your abilities." He scanned the countertops. They were covered in prep items. The storm before the calm. Lee used to get frustrated with the mess she created before a dinner party, but she'd always pulled it together in the end. Come to think of it, Lee's doubts about her capabilities had hurt, too. At least Finn's were warranted because he knew next to nothing about her.

"It's like checking out a painting before it's finished. It's not going to resemble anything right now, but tomorrow night, it will."

"Okay." Finn raised palms. "I'm here if you need me to do anything. Otherwise, I'll stay out of it."

"Thank you." Ivy appreciated that. Because she planned to show Finn that he hadn't made a mistake in working out a deal with her. That she was still the capable woman she'd once been. That she remembered how to make decisions and be confident in them. And that maybe her instincts didn't have to be wrong all the time—the way they had been with Lee.

Actually…most of that she needed to prove to herself. For Finn, this was just about a dinner party.

For Ivy, it was about so much more.

Having Ivy orchestrate the dinner couldn't be worse than anything Finn would have managed to accomplish.

At least that was what he told himself while moving cattle the day of the gathering.

He'd stayed out of Ivy's way and out of the house on purpose, because she'd been right last night. He hadn't trusted her to handle things. Pretty sure the seed of that was watered by Chrissa. How had one woman done such a number on him in such a short amount of time?

The crazy part was, despite the way Chrissa had twisted things and confused him, commandeering his help and then reneging on everything they'd talked about, Finn had still struggled to let go of her, to leave her behind and move on with his life. Not because he couldn't stop loving her, although that had taken some effort on his part, but more because he was worried about her. Worried that the stories she'd told him about her ex/current husband *were* true, and that the man had somehow talked her out of trusting her instincts.

But Finn couldn't save Chrissa. She'd made her choice, and he'd had to walk away. And that had messed with him. It also explained why he was so concerned about the deal he'd made with Ivy.

He'd engaged with her girls yesterday without thinking, and it had come back to haunt him. He was starting to entertain questions like…were they going to be okay? Would they make it to California safely after her vehicle was fixed? How would the girls fare without a father in their lives?

Things he had no business fretting about.

Things that reminded him that he shouldn't have made the deal in the first place. But it was too late to change anything now. The dinner would be happening in just over an hour, and in a couple of days, Ivy would get her vehicle back and she'd be on her way to California. Then Finn could put an end to any thoughts of her or her girls needing rescuing.

Not that Ivy had even asked him for that. At least she'd come up with the idea of them making a trade. Which meant Finn wasn't rescuing her. He wasn't pulling another Chrissa or repeating the past.

Finn strode from the barn to the house. The triplets were outside, playing with the babysitter. A girl Charlie had recommended. She'd said that Ivy would need someone to watch the girls for the evening if she was going to be able to host. Ivy had agreed, and the two of them had worked out the rest of the details. Finn would write the check at the end of the night, and as long as the dinner went well, it would be worth it.

The girls waved and called out to him. He returned the greeting and then paused with his hand on the outside doorknob. *I should have come back earlier. Checked on things.*

But I promised I wouldn't do exactly that.

If the house wasn't ready, he would be scrambling, big-time. And based on the mess Ivy had created while getting ready… Finn opened the front door with a wince already in place, but any concern quickly fell away.

The house was immaculate, but more than that, it didn't even look like his place.

The lights had been dimmed, and flickering candlelight filled the living room, island and dining table. The island had been set up as a serving station, and the plates and napkins were ready to go. They'd discussed that there wouldn't be enough chairs for everyone to have a seat at the table, but Ivy had remedied that by placing white folding chairs throughout the living room in addition to the usual seating. Finn wasn't sure where she'd commandeered those—if she'd rented or borrowed or what—but she'd told him she'd stuck to the budget, so he didn't really care how she'd made it happen.

The place smelled amazing, too. Garlic, potato, simmering barbecued beef all came rushing toward him, and… Was that fresh bread? His taste buds ignited.

Finn shut the door behind him and strolled toward the island, where a note stuck amid the tableware caught his eye.

Getting ready. Be back soon. Ivy.

After showering off the grime and dirt from the day, Finn dressed in his best jeans and an off-white button-down shirt Charlie had gotten him for his birthday when he'd turned twenty-nine last month. She'd be thirty-one in a few weeks. They were just over two years apart, and their mom had often teased them that they were so close in age it had been like raising twins. Now that Finn had been introduced to Ivy's triplets, he'd have to argue with her over that. Three at the same age was a whole other level.

He slid on his good boots—the ones not covered in manure and snowmelt—and returned to the kitchen. Ivy still wasn't back, so he poked around at the food options she'd set up. The fridge was full of items he didn't remember purchasing. She must have filled in or made something better out of his supplies.

About fifteen minutes before guests were supposed to arrive, Finn panicked. Ivy still wasn't back. Was there a problem with the girls and the sitter? Should he shoot her a text? They'd exchanged numbers this week while figuring out details for tonight. Or should he walk over to the bunkhouse and check on her?

If she didn't return, could he figure out the food?

The front door flew open and Ivy flew in. She'd gone from pretty—he wasn't going to deny the woman had the kind of face that got him right in the gut—to stunning. Her makeup was perfect—not too much, not too little. The color lining her lids was shimmery and captivating, making her eyes pop, and her cheeks were either flushed or she'd added some pink, because they were kissable and distracting.

She spotted him and flashed a smile. "Hey! Were you worried I wasn't coming back? You really need to work on your trust issues, Finn Brightwood." And then she laughed as if teasing him. Little did she know how close to the bull's-eye her dart had just landed.

"I'm working on it." Among other things. Finn motioned to the room. "It looks great in here." The candles were fake; he could see that now. Safer, and they still cast a nice glow.

"Thank you. It's a great space, so that made it easy."

Easy. Maybe for her. Definitely not for him. "What can I do to help?"

She rounded the island, then handed him a serving tray and motioned to the clear cups. "Fill those with the sparkling cider. I'm going to have some poured and ready because usually everyone arrives at the same time and then things get crazy and people get missed. Don't want that happening."

A knock sounded on the front door, and Charlie poked her head inside. "It's me."

"Yay!" Ivy's delight at seeing his sister made Finn's chest squeeze with an unknown emotion. "I didn't know you were coming tonight, Charlie."

"She was included in the numbers because when she

heard the cattlemen's group had lured me into hosting, she wanted to attend so that she could see me fail."

Charlie removed her coat and opened the front closet. "Now, Finn, that's not true." She spun in their direction after hanging her coat. "Okay, maybe it is true." Her gaze met Ivy's, and they both laughed.

"I suddenly feel very ganged-up-on."

The women hugged in greeting, and Charlie started an inquisition right after. "How's your head? Anything new? Any reason for me to regret not shoving you into the ambulance the other night?"

Ivy grabbed a bottle of cider from the fridge and handed it to Finn. "Nope. Nothing new. I've been having some headaches, but they've been minor. The girls all seem fine, too."

In minutes, the doorbell rang, and people started arriving. Ivy was right—it was busy. The drinks Finn had poured disappeared quickly. Ivy had set out some appetizers. Guests mingled and snacked while waiting for everyone to arrive. There were lots of comments about how nice his house looked, how great everything smelled.

Ivy dashed around in a casual burgundy dress that belted at her waist, making sure drinks were filled, chatting with everyone. At one point, Finn overheard someone asking how she knew him. She said they were friends, then moved the conversation along, questioning how long they'd been ranching, exclaiming over the length of time.

She could host parties as a profession.

Once everyone arrived, Finn prayed over the food and people began dishing up plates. Ivy didn't slow down for a second. She stationed herself behind the island, keeping a hawkeyed lookout on anything that had emptied or was starting to run low. Numerous times during the evening, Finn found his attention straying in her direction. She was…distracting.

Finn directed his focus to C. C. Leap instead. The old rancher was known for his expertise in land replenishing. Finn had plenty of questions to ask him, since he felt the Burkes had overused the land, and that had been part of what led to their downfall. He didn't want to be prideful about his theories. He wanted to ask a competent source about rejuvenating the ranch.

C.C. offered to meet with him and analyze the ranch, which Finn considered a victory so big he'd host this silly dinner all over again if it netted him the same results.

By the time everyone had finished the main course, Finn had been told no less than five times that he was throwing the best dinner party the group had attended. They also recommended he plan on hosting next year's, since he'd done such a good job. Finn resisted groaning at that. *He* hadn't done anything. Ivy had managed it all.

And to think he'd doubted her for even a second. Just went to show how far down his trust-meter had fallen. And how far back up it would have to go in order to be in working condition again.

Chapter Three

The last guests left around nine in the evening, and Finn blew out a sigh of relief as the door closed behind them.

Everything had gone well, and he was as done as a forgotten burger on the grill. The temptation to crawl into bed and crash and not deal with the mess the group had created was strong, but Finn resisted. Better to knock it out now. Besides, Ivy had been cleaning up throughout the evening when the opportunity allowed, so it shouldn't take too long.

The guests had loved her. More than one rancher had commented on Finn having a great girlfriend, that he'd found a keeper. At first Finn had corrected them. He'd explained that he and Ivy were friends, sticking to the story she'd given earlier in the evening, though new acquaintances was a better description.

But by the fourth remark, Finn had given up. Trying to explain why a beautiful woman was helping him host wasn't getting him anywhere. At the next gathering, he'd just tell the group that he and Ivy had broken up. It would be easier than trying to clarify their relationship.

Finn gathered used cups and tossed them into the trash, the house eerily quiet. Where was Ivy? Had she gone back to the bunkhouse? It would be strange that she hadn't let him know. Especially since he needed to pay the sitter. Not that Finn had expected her to stay until the end of the evening. She'd more than surpassed his expectations throughout the night.

Finn checked down the hall and found the bathroom door open. She wasn't in there. As he passed by the den that was tucked behind the kitchen, he paused in the doorway. A dainty form was sitting on the couch, head back, eyes closed. Ivy's steady breathing told him she'd conked out. A strange, troubling warmth swirled inside his chest.

Good thing she's leaving after the weekend. Doug had thought her car would be done on Monday. Finn was starting to think Monday wasn't soon enough.

What was it with him and rescuing women? Ivy had been through a lot in her life… Finn would even go so far as to say her current situation registered at hot mess levels. Her husband had not only embezzled, he'd taken his own life. She was moving her girls across the country to live with her parents and start over.

The last thing he needed was to get involved, so he was actually grateful their deal was coming to an end.

He shifted his weight, and the floor creaked beneath him. Ivy shot awake, her hand fluttering to her chest.

"Oh, no. I can't believe I fell asleep." Panic tugged on her features, and she began pushing up from the cushions.

"Don't get up." He stepped into the room. "I mean, don't get up too quickly." It was likely that the accident was still taking a toll on her body.

Finn moved to the chair across from her and eased onto the cushion, as exhausted as he would be after manual labor. He turned on the lamp on the side table next to him, causing a yellow glow to illuminate a slice of the room.

"Sorry I missed the last part. I assume everyone is gone?"

"The house is empty, thankfully, and you didn't miss anything. Sending a few people out the door was no big deal and not what you signed up for. I thought you'd cover the food for tonight and that's it. But you went above and beyond that. You were a *really* great host. I'm going to have a problem because of what an amazing job you did."

Her brow furrowed. "Why's that?"

"A number of people already suggested that I host next year, too. Said it was the best annual dinner they'd had in a decade." Finn had wondered if those comments were overheard by some of the others in the room who'd hosted previously, but everyone seemed so happy to give up the job that nobody had claimed offense.

The compliment flushed Ivy's cheeks. "Guess you'll have to recruit someone else to help out then."

"They won't do as good a job as you."

"No." The bow of her lips increased. "They won't."

"I gather your head has been bothering you more than you've let on." All week Finn had been wondering if Ivy should be doing so much. Now he had his answer.

"It's been pesky, but nothing a little medicine can't help."

"I have a hard time believing you right now."

Ivy's fingers twisted on her lap. "Well, what was I going to do? Crawl into bed and not get out? What would the girls have done if I was out of commission? Sometimes as a mom, you've just got to…do. There isn't a choice."

And Finn was almost certain she'd had to do the same, even while married. But he didn't plan to ask about what kind of spouse and father her late husband had been, because he could guess the answer, and because he wasn't going *there* with Ivy.

The only place he was going with Ivy was separate directions. Even if hosting this dinner with her had turned out to be a pleasant surprise. Because there was a whole lot of difference between one week of agreement…and another rescue.

Ivy signed the paperwork to pick up her vehicle and grasped the key in her hand. Freedom. Finally. Not having access to her Suburban had been a lesson in patience that she hadn't agreed to participate in. The idea that she could roll out of the lot and go anywhere, do anything, made her feel as if a load of bricks had been removed from her handbag.

She'd been dependent on other people since she and the girls had slid off the road. Namely the Brightwood siblings. She'd fought hard to regain her independence after losing Lee—and herself over the years—so the setback had been a struggle.

Ivy loaded new car seats and the girls into the vehicle, then made her way toward Charlie's Garage. The other woman had given them a ride to the auto body shop and then asked if Ivy would stop by the unfinished café she was opening, which was next door to her mechanic shop. Why, Ivy wasn't sure, but Charlie had been there for them the past week, even going so far as to lend Ivy and the girls bedding, towels and other supplies for the bunkhouse, so she would never consider not granting the small request, even with three distractions in tow.

As if to emphasize her thoughts, the girls' volume upped in the back seat as they squabbled over a doll.

The sign at the front of the café matched the vintage style of the one over Charlie's Garage. Charlie's Pit Stop. Cute. Charlie had told Ivy the place was meant to be a spot for garage customers to grab a cup of coffee or a pastry while they waited for their car to be fixed as well as a spot for Westbend residents to meet up or grab some light fare.

Ivy parked near the front entrance. She let the girls out on the sidewalk, and they ran ahead, looping back when Ivy opened the café door for them. Inside, the last remnants of construction dust floated in the sunshine. The brick wall and worn wooden floors screamed original, but the counter, cabinets and shelves lining the right side were definitely new. It was a great mix of retro and redone.

Footsteps sounded from a back hallway, and then Charlie appeared. "Hi, guys! I'm so glad you stopped by. Any chance you girls want to check out my sandbox out back?" Charlie's gaze shot to Ivy. "Sorry—I should have asked you first. But I have something to talk to you about, so I thought maybe the distraction would give us a second. Is that okay?"

"Please!" the triplets chorused, and Ivy conceded. The drive from Connecticut had been long, and they'd been loving the freedom to play this week.

Nerves kicked up in Ivy's stomach as she and the girls followed Charlie through the back hallway and out an exit, then walked the few steps over to the sandbox. What did Charlie want to talk to her about?

The triplets settled in quickly, using the dump truck and buckets to begin building. Spring in Colorado, Ivy was learning, could mean snow or sunshine. Warm, like today, when the sun felt like a massage against her skin, or freezing, like last week, when the weather had been spitting snow faster than imaginable.

Charlie motioned to the small patio table and chairs, and they moved to sit. Ivy threaded and unthreaded her fingers on her lap while she waited for Charlie to speak.

"I don't know exactly how to broach this, but I'm wondering if you'll consider something."

"Okay." Ivy stretched out the word, her mind overflowing with questions regarding what Charlie would say next.

"I'll give you a little backstory. I've been looking for a manager for the café for a while. Someone with experience to handle the setup, the opening and the staff. And I found the perfect person. Only about three weeks ago, she changed her mind. She'd been planning to move to Westbend for the job, but after visiting, she decided it was too small-town. She's a city girl, and she couldn't make the switch."

"I'm sorry. That sounds stressful."

Charlie's sigh was like an exclamation point. "Tell me about it. I have a shop to run, and I love being a mechanic. I have no interest in managing the café myself. I'd always planned to hire out that position. Since she changed her mind, I've been scrambling for a replacement for her. We're supposed to open in a little over five weeks, and there's no way that can happen if

I don't find someone immediately. Which is where you come into the picture."

"Me?" What did Ivy have to do with any of this?

"I saw what you did at Finn's the other night. You handled the dinner and made it look easy. You're a natural. I know you and the girls are heading to your parents' home in California, and I'm not asking you not to do that. I'm just asking if you'd consider postponing your departure a bit in order to stay in Westbend and orchestrate the setup of the café."

Somewhere during Charlie's spiel, Ivy's jaw had dropped open. "You want me? But I don't have any experience doing something like that. I'm not qualified at all."

"Sometimes a line on a résumé isn't where it's at. You handled so much at Finn's in a week, all while recovering from the accident. You're more than capable. And I also paid the woman I was going to hire to outline a café setup plan for me. I have all of the details of what needs to happen and when in order to get the café functioning. I just need someone qualified to implement it."

Wow. For so long Ivy had felt inept. She'd been a stay-at-home mom, which she'd loved, and she'd worked a few hours a week at a boutique clothing store. Just to get out of the house and stash a bit of money aside for a rainy day. Ivy had sensed something was going on with Lee, but she hadn't known what. He'd teased her about her job, thinking that she'd traded her paychecks for clothing, but she hadn't. Ivy had saved that money, and now it was getting her and the girls across the country.

To think that Charlie saw something in her that she no longer believed existed was a huge boost.

Charlie outlined what she could pay Ivy, which was

generous but not outrageous. "And if you and the girls continue to stay in the bunkhouse, then your expenses wouldn't be that much." The bunkhouse was cozy. Sure, it didn't have a kitchen, but Ivy could get by with a microwave or a toaster oven. Something to make the situation livable.

Wait—am I actually considering this? The idea is wild. Who would watch the girls? And how could I afford anyone for that?

Her parents would think she was losing her mind for even contemplating it. They were all set to rescue her and the girls…just like Dad had probably assumed they would need to the moment she'd gone against his advice and married Lee.

Continuing to California made the most sense and was best for the girls' future. Wasn't it?

"If you could stay a week past the café opening, the staff should be trained by then, and it would give me time to find a new manager. And if you decide to take me up on my offer, I'll be able to provide you with a reference. I'm sure starting over is tough, and I thought that might be a help to you."

A reference, even from that short amount of time, would be amazing.

And the chance to earn money doing something she'd no doubt enjoy was tempting. She also wasn't in a desperate rush to get to her parents' house. She'd talked to her mom this morning, and the woman was already planning various lessons for the girls. Horseback riding. Swimming. Tennis at the country club. She'd even put them on the waiting list for a prestigious preschool that Ivy wasn't sure she wanted them to attend. The conversation had made her hyperventilate and get off the phone as quickly as possible.

Would it be so terrible to delay their next step? Their next long-drawn-out step. Because Ivy wouldn't be able to afford moving the girls out of her parents' house for a long time. Especially not in Southern California, where prices were astronomical.

"But what about the girls? How can I work and watch them? That's not fair to you, so I'd have to find someone to babysit. And there's three of them. It would be too expensive."

Charlie's lips pressed tight and then curved. "I *may* have taken the liberty of asking Ms. Lina, an older, retired woman from church who loves kids, if she'd consider watching them. It's not set in stone, but I knew you'd have that question, and I wanted to see if there was an answer before I even offered you the job. If you're interested, I can introduce you to her and you can decide. She said she doesn't need much in terms of money."

"The girls went to Sunday school yesterday, and I'm pretty sure Ms. Lina was their teacher. They adored her." Finn had offered them a ride to church on Sunday, and Ivy had accepted, needing the reminder and encouragement in her faith. Ms. Lina had been fabulous. Even in that short amount of time, she'd doted on the girls. They'd come home talking about the woman on repeat.

"Yes! She does teach Sunday school. That's her." Charlie leaned forward. "I know this is a lot to dump on you, and I understand if you're not interested. You can tell me no and I'll stop talking about it. No hard feelings. I just had to ask. Ever since I met you, I couldn't shake the feeling that you were meant to be here. Even if it's just for a short while."

Wow. Ivy would never have thought something like this was even possible. She'd assumed that she'd been out of the workforce for so long that she didn't have any skills to offer anyone. That was why she and the girls were moving in the first place. She'd needed a cushion—some time to find work and re-qualify herself. But if what Charlie was offering was legit, and from the short time she'd known the woman, Ivy imagined it was, then that meant she wasn't without any skills. That meant hosting that dinner the other night wasn't something every person could do. And setting up the café…that sounded more like playing than like work.

"I think… I'm not uninterested." Charlie beamed at her confession. "Have you talked to Finn about us staying in the bunkhouse? What does he want me to pay in rent?"

Charlie grinned like a cat who'd found a bowl of cream. "If you're actually considering it, then don't worry about my brother. You just leave that part up to me."

In the barn, Finn tinkered with a piece of broken loading chute as he heard a vehicle approach the ranch and then slow down.

Ivy and the girls.

Charlie had picked them up today to help Ivy get her SUV back. Everything must have gone according to plan. Good. That meant she and the triplets would be moving on, continuing their trek. And Finn's life could return to normal.

The thought left him lonely and relieved all at the

same time. He'd grown used to the girls' chatter and found them more amusing than he cared to admit. The place would definitely be quiet after they were gone.

Finn walked out of the barn to see that not only was Ivy back, but his sister had followed her here. Her Toyota FJ Cruiser was parked right behind Ivy. Strange. Was Charlie concerned about something mechanical being wrong with Ivy's vehicle? Or maybe she'd come to help them pack up. Although…he doubted they'd brought that much into the bunkhouse.

The girls piled out of the Suburban and immediately began a game of tag, chasing each other, giggling over everything. Finn's mouth curved. He certainly wished them well and hoped that the next portion of their young lives went better than the first.

Ivy and Charlie approached him together, and Finn's intuition sparked. Something was going on.

"What's up? I see the Suburban is back in working order." Ivy nodded, looking more unsure than since he'd met her. "Everything okay?"

"Everything is great," Charlie piped in. "Ivy just agreed to stay for six weeks to help me open the café."

Wait. What? Finn knew that Charlie's hired manager had flaked on her, and that she'd been scrambling to find someone else, but what did Ivy have to do with the price of eggs?

"Since Ivy hosted your dinner and did such a great job, I basically begged her to consider staying. I think she has what it takes to get the café running."

"That's…great." Finn almost swallowed his tongue trying to eke out the words. *Just because she's in town doesn't mean she's in your life. Relax.* "Congratulations, Ivy."

"Thank you." She'd transformed into a meek version of herself. Definitely not the woman who'd asked him for a trade regarding Saturday's dinner.

Why did Finn feel like he was missing something?

"I told Ivy that since no one is using the bunkhouse, you'd be fine with her and the girls continuing to stay there."

What? Why hadn't Charlie asked him about Ivy staying when it was just the two of them? But even if she had, what would he say? Finn had no desire to get into the reasons behind his why. Charlie didn't know everything that had happened in North Dakota, and he was nowhere near ready to divulge the details to her. The whole situation with Chrissa still wounded him on a soul-deep level. It was as if he'd failed—at saving her, at having a successful relationship, at moving past all of it once everything was over and done.

"I'll pay rent." Ivy the negotiator was back. "It's more than you were getting with it just sitting empty."

"The bunkhouse isn't finished. There's no way I can accept rent." In fact… "Shouldn't it have a certificate of occupancy or something like that? I doubt anyone should be living there, temporary or not." Which could be his ticket out.

"That's why I'm thinking you don't charge Ivy and the girls for staying there," Charlie responded. "It's not like you need it, and as she pointed out, it's just sitting empty otherwise."

Ivy squeaked. "Charlie, you never said anything about not paying rent."

Charlie lifted her shoulders, the picture of innocence. "Finn's right. He can't take money for something that's not finished. So let's just consider you and the girls living in the bunkhouse as a draw for you staying to open the café."

Finn's chest itched to explode. He wanted to live on *his* ranch alone. He didn't want Ivy and her three girls there. He didn't want to feel anything they might make him feel. And he definitely didn't want to get drawn into another rescue.

But what was he supposed to do? If he said no, he was a jerk. He didn't have an explanation he was willing to share with these two. Not without giving away just how much the Chrissa situation had messed with him.

A wail sounded from one of the girls, and the adults' attention jumped in that direction. Reese had fallen during their game and was now sprawled on the dirt. Sage and Lola were bent over her. From the chatter Finn could catch, it sounded as if they were partially checking on their sister and partially arguing over whose fault the injury was.

Ivy jogged over to triage the situation, leaving Finn with his sister.

"Why would you drop something like this on me in front of Ivy?"

"I never thought you'd even have to think about it. This is what we do—this is how Granddad taught us to be. And Mom and Dad, too, for that matter." His sister was pulling in the big guns. Their granddad was a man Finn strove to emulate. At ninety-six and still in excellent condition, Marshall Brightwood was wise and strong and gentle all at the same time. And yes, he would lend a hand to Ivy and her girls without hesitation. The old version of Finn would have done the same. But he was stuck in a new world—one he hadn't experienced before—and he wasn't sure how to get out. Or if he even wanted out.

Charlie's eyes morphed to slits of concern. "Finn, what is going on with you?" Her voice registered at just above whispering-in-church levels. With Ivy's current distraction, there was no way she could overhear. "Ever since you moved back you haven't been yourself. It's like something in North Dakota broke you, and you're just not the same. And if I had to guess, it has something to do with the woman you were seeing there." Charlie paused as if to let him fill in details, but he stayed silent.

His sister had started dating Ryker Hayes last fall, so she wasn't in the headspace to understand his current headspace. She was in love, and Finn didn't want to touch that emotion with a ten-foot pole.

"I miss that old version of my brother." Her demeanor softened. "Is he ever coming back? Are you going to be okay?"

He blinked away a flash of emotion. "I'm fine. Or at least I will be. Just give me some time, okay?" He wished he knew how long it would take to turn back into himself, because he'd like an answer to that also.

"It's not like Ivy and the girls will be in your space if they stay in the bunkhouse. She'll be working in town. You'll hardly see them."

"There's no kitchen in it, so if she needs to cook, she'll be in mine."

And now he sounded like a brat.

"I'll help her get a small fridge and microwave. And a hot plate. That way she can make whatever for the girls at the bunkhouse, and she's not invading your world. Having Ivy and the girls stay here will be a massive help for me. You know how I've been struggling to find a manager since the other one changed her mind."

Yeah, he knew. "I'm sorry that I can't explain my reservations. You're just going to have to trust that I'm not trying to be a jerk. I just… This isn't my first choice."

Charlie's fingers jutted through her short red locks. "I'd put them up in my apartment if I could, but it's too small for that many people. Ivy and the girls wouldn't even fit in the second bedroom together. Are you going to make me find them somewhere else to live? Because you know that's not going to be easy. Not for such a short amount of time. Which means she likely won't stay then, and I'll be back to square one."

And how could he do that to his sister? Charlie was obviously desperate for this. Ivy wanted it, too. Finn was the only one holding out.

"Fine. Do what you need to do, Char. It's only for six weeks."

And Finn wouldn't get involved in Ivy or the girls' plight during that time.

At least…not any more than he was already getting roped into.

Chapter Four

The 6 a.m. start time for men's Bible study was always painful and always worth it. Today's focus on First Thessalonians had been about giving thanks in all circumstances. Finn had winced so many times during the teaching that Ryker had shot him a "what's up with you" look from across the table.

He definitely hadn't expressed thanks to God yesterday after being ambushed by Charlie and Ivy.

Or this morning when he'd woken up.

Once the study ended, some of the men took off for work while others stayed to catch up. Finn waved goodbye across the room to Luc Wilder, who he'd worked for at Wilder Guest Ranch, then met up with Ryker and Evan Hawke by the coffeepot.

Ryker had started dating Charlie last fall after she'd fostered his niece. At first Finn had been wary of the situation, worried about Ryker hurting his sister. But eventually he'd warmed up to the other man's presence in Charlie's life. A good thing since he didn't have any choice in the matter. Ryker and Charlie were not only really happy together, but extremely supportive of each other. And now that Ryker's sister, Kaia, had regained custody of her five-year-old daughter, Honor, they were both still involved in the girl's life.

Ryker's eyes crinkled with humor as he refilled the paper coffee cup with dark roast. "Did I see you struggling to give thanks during Bible study because you have some guests staying on your property for the time being?"

The sigh that ripped from Finn's chest was agitated. "Something like that. This is my sister's fault, and since you two are joined at the hip, that pretty much makes it your fault, too. You could have stepped in and stopped her. Or at least given me a heads-up so that I could have had my defense ready."

"Charlie's been so busy between the garage and the café that I didn't even know what she was up to until it was done. Sorry, man."

Evan grabbed one of the leftover breakfast pastries and a napkin. He was married to Charlie's good friend Addie, who ran the Little Red Hen Bed & Breakfast. "This is how rumors get started. Ivy and the girls staying on your ranch equals the town having you two married by summer."

"Fall at the latest," Ryker added gravely.

"Why give it so long? Why don't we just elope right now?" Both men laughed at Finn's outburst. "Just because you two are crazy in love doesn't mean everyone has to be. What in the world is wrong with being single? Huh? I've got a ranch to focus on." Regret walloped Finn like a rogue fly ball. He'd been so sidelined by the Ivy stuff that he'd forgotten his plan to talk to Gage Frasier after study. "I meant to catch Gage this morning. I have some questions for him about summer calving."

Evan tsked. "Changing the subject. Denial is the first sign."

"That it is," Ryker agreed.

Finn stifled a groan since it would only fuel their amusement. "Ivy and the girls aren't staying that long, so hopefully by the time the town figures out they're here, they'll already be gone." He hadn't even thought to be concerned about the rumor mill, but Evan was right. It would explode with new kindling. "And I appreciate you giving me something else to worry about."

Ryker slapped him on the back. "It'll go by quick. It's just a month, right? And you know Charlie is desperate for the help."

"Six weeks." As long as nothing else changed. And yes, Finn knew. "I don't suppose Addie has some room for Ivy and her girls at the B & B. Come to think of it, that's a great idea. Why can't they squat there instead of at my place?"

"I'm not in charge of reservations," Evan responded, "but I think the B & B is out of Ivy's price range. Which is why she and the girls ended up at your ranch."

True. And for that reason, Finn should be fine letting her use the bunkhouse. It wasn't of value to him in its unfinished state. If he hadn't been so blindsided by Chrissa in North Dakota, he likely wouldn't have thought twice about the situation with Ivy. He would have said yes in a heartbeat. But as Charlie had pointed out, that version of him had disappeared, and he wasn't sure when the old Finn planned to return, if ever.

Thankfully, their conversation switched to catching up on other news. Evan was booking out expeditions for the summer. After he'd had a below-the-knee amputation in high school, he'd gained firsthand experience with the kind of effort it took to recover from a trauma. Now he and his partner led groups of trauma victims on Colorado expeditions as they pushed boundaries and found healing.

Ryker had found employment at Sunny Farms Horse Ranch when he'd moved to Colorado and claimed it was his dream job working with horses and teens.

And Finn, after a stint at Wilder Guest Ranch, had fallen for Westbend and worked for years on an oil rig in order to save up the money for his own spread.

He would say they'd all found their perfect careers—something he could and did give thanks for.

Usually Finn enjoyed the drive home from the early morning Bible study. The sun as it hung low, waking the world. The stretch of his land as it came into view and the way the mountains circled the ranch. The snow-capped peaks like live artwork that changed every day. But this morning, as he returned to the ranch and spotted Ivy's Suburban parked outside the bunkhouse, his stomach soured.

Give thanks in all *things.*

Yeah, yeah. I'm working on it.

Knowing to do something and accomplishing it were two very different issues.

Finn managed to get away from the house and out on the ranch without running into Ivy or the girls. In the last week, calves had begun dropping. He checked on the new arrivals until around late morning, when his ranch hand was set to arrive. He'd been operating minimally since a few ranch hands had left when the Burkes sold. Cliff and Behr were both part-timers. Cliff was in high school and helped around his class schedule. Behr had worked for the Burkes but was close to retirement. He'd gone down to part-time after they'd sold, and Finn had been making do with the bare-bones staff while deciding how much help he needed.

He returned to the house to meet Cliff and instead came across Ivy moving items from her Suburban into the bunkhouse. Charlie had told him she was taking the day to get settled and would start work tomorrow.

Finn bounced his eyes elsewhere.

She's not yours to take care of. Let her be. Let her figure things out on her own, and whatever you do, stay out of it.

Ivy yelped just as he neared the front door of the house. Finn spun to check on her. The box in her hands had dropped to the ground and split open. Contents were everywhere.

He threw a silent I-don't-wanna hissy fit. Why couldn't he have just gotten out of here before seeing that?

No matter how much Finn wanted to march the other direction and leave Ivy to her own devices, he could not. It wasn't in him to turn away from someone in need, even when he was desperate to learn how to do exactly that.

When he reached Ivy, he knelt alongside her and began picking up pieces of the girls' clothing. Spring could bring rain, snow, wind and anything in between, and the ground was a mess.

"Do you want to separate out the clean from the dirty?" What landed on top was probably still okay.

Ivy gave a frustrated exhale. "Yes. Thanks."

She retrieved a garbage bag from the bunkhouse,

and they sorted pieces, tossing the dirty into the bag and the clean onto the seat of the Suburban.

"You can use my washer and dryer for this stuff." He'd thought about her needing his kitchen on occasion but hadn't considered the laundry room. That necessity would probably far outweigh the other, especially with three little girls. Finn forced his tongue to function. "Anytime you need it. It's no big deal. The laundry room is next to the main bathroom."

The words came out, but they were clipped and short, like a child who'd decided to cut their own nails. Finn was doing his best to hide his frustration at Ivy's presence, but at the moment, his best was pretty pathetic.

"That's okay. I can go to the Laundromat in town." She paused in the middle of sorting. "There has to be one in Westbend, doesn't there?"

There was, but having her lug everything into town would be about the most unchristian thing Finn could do to the woman. Laundry for the triplets had to be a beast.

"There's no need. I'm out of the house a lot of the time anyway, so if you'd rather not run into me, you can just pop over when I'm not there."

"Finn, I'm not trying to avoid you."

Right. He was the one doing that with her. Talk about giving himself away.

"Okay, then. Anytime is fine." He tossed the last dirty item into the bag and stood. "What else is going inside?" He motioned to her Suburban.

"Nothing I can't handle. I'll get the rest."

His feet stayed planted in a wide stance.

Give thanks in all things.

God, thank You that Ivy and the girls are only staying six more weeks.

An internal buzzer sounded as if shouting that his prayer had been dead wrong.

Thank You that I get to go feed cattle in a minute and get out of here?

Another buzzer.

Finn was going to have to work on his gratefulness since he was currently failing the school of First Thessalonians miserably.

"What else?" He motioned to the Suburban again. He'd come this far. He might as well finish.

"All of it." Ivy's whisper was a mix of concern and defiance. As if daring him to disagree with her. He didn't plan to. He didn't plan to talk at all.

Finn got to work. He didn't care what was in the boxes or why she wanted them all inside.

It wasn't his place to ask questions. Not when he was choosing not to care about the answers.

Ivy was going to go out on a limb and guess that Finn wasn't pleased with something. And if she went even further out on that same limb, she would guess it had something to do with her and her girls staying in the bunkhouse.

If Finn was so upset about them being here, why had he agreed to Charlie's plan in the first place?

Was his irritation because Ivy wasn't paying rent? She couldn't imagine that was the issue. Finn hadn't been making money on the bunkhouse; nor would he if she wasn't here. Not with the kitchen being unfinished. And he'd never mentioned the desire to continue the construction the Burkes had started.

Maybe he was just introverted and craved his own space. Ivy could understand that. But once she started working, it was quite possible she and Finn could go days without running into each other.

So what was under his collar? When he'd returned from being out on the ranch a bit ago and stomped off to his house without so much as a hello, Ivy had experienced a tinge of concern.

Then she'd dropped the box, and he'd come running—begrudgingly. If he was going to be so persnickety while helping her out, she wished he had just kept walking.

Finn entered the bunkhouse and settled one box on top of another. He studied the stack she'd begun in the open space the kitchen cabinets would have occupied, but if he harbored concerns, he didn't voice them.

"Thank you for your help, but I can get the rest. I'm sure you have plenty to do."

Ivy had heard rumblings that ranching season in the spring was hectic and busy. Finn certainly had more pressing matters to attend to.

"I'm good." He exited the bunkhouse, and air leaked from her lungs. What a mess. When Finn and Charlie had decided she couldn't or shouldn't pay rent, Ivy had been upset. She didn't want charity. She wanted to prove she was capable of taking care of her girls without handouts. And since money was off the table, she had to find a way to show Finn that she wasn't freeloading. That she could be of assistance to him, too, and not just the other way around.

The girls were now playing outside, enjoying the crisp spring weather and the so-close-you-could-almost-touch-it sunshine. When a truck engine rumbled onto ranch property, Ivy checked out the window to make sure they weren't in harm's way.

They were off to the left, nowhere near the vehicle.

Finn received something from the delivery truck, his greeting to the driver friendly and welcoming.

The man was confusing. Generous one second, irritated the next. He was tall—maybe six-two—and broad-shouldered. Whenever Ivy caught a glimpse of him, her insides gave a shimmy of attraction and recognition, as if to remind her that even though she was a mom of three three-year-olds, she was still a woman... and there was nothing wrong with her vision.

Finn had looked good the night of the cattlemen's dinner in a simple button-down shirt and jeans. He looked good when he donned his hat and jacket and headed out on the ranch.

The man was like a Western ad and even included the serious smolder.

The good news about planning to move into her parents' house with the girls after helping open the café was that she wouldn't be in Westbend long enough to act on any undesirable attraction to Finn. Their short stop in Colorado wouldn't amount to enough time to figure out who Finn was on the inside, and the outside wasn't enough. Ivy had moved too fast with Lee, and she wouldn't be making that mistake again. Certainly not with three little girls to raise. She had to be the example, and she couldn't fail them like she had with their father.

Ivy moved into the bedroom and studied the dresser. Six drawers. She'd have to get creative on space. She'd also have to clean the bag full of clothes that had fallen in the mud, but they could manage for now. Especially since neither the idea of the Laundromat in town nor using Finn's facilities brought any excitement. Thankfully, she'd packed clothes, toys and other necessities in her vehicle while sending what she'd hoped would be less important items in the portable storage container that had already arrived at her parents' place. While they certainly didn't have everything they'd need, they had enough to get by for six more weeks.

Ivy hadn't included professional clothing items in the Suburban, so she'd be rotating through jeans and her best shirts plus a few sweaters for work at the café. Charlie hadn't had any issue with that when she'd broached the subject with her.

Ivy sorted for almost twenty minutes before realizing she didn't hear the girls' chatter.

Panic zipped along her spine, and she rushed to the open front door. She didn't spot them, so she stepped outside, calling their names. When no one answered her, she jogged toward the barn. The girls had an infatuation with animals of all kinds, so it was likely they'd wandered there.

Ivy stepped inside, her lungs functioning again when she spotted three blond heads bent over something. Finn was with them. Reese had copped a seat on the ground, which equaled more laundry, but they were all present and safe, so Ivy would worry about that another day.

She inched closer. They were pulling baby chicks out of a box. Finn was showing the girls how to help the chicks drink water and eat, and then they were depositing them inside a squared-off area with wooden sides. A heat lamp was clipped to one of the short walls, and a few chicks were waddling around on newspapers laid out inside.

Sage deposited one in the holding area. Before her fingers could go into her mouth, Finn reached out, lightning-fast and yet gentle, stopping the movement.

"You can't touch the chicks and then put your fingers in your mouth." He glanced at Reese and Lola to make sure they were listening. "And don't kiss them, either. They can make people sick. So only hold them in your hands and then don't touch your mouth. Sage—" his voice was serious as a heart attack "—can you promise me you won't put your fingers in your mouth? Because otherwise you can't touch the chicks."

Sage nodded vigorously.

"And after we teach them to eat and drink, we're going to wash our hands really, *really* well. I probably should have asked your mom before I let you girls do this at all."

Ivy's heart hiccupped at the kindness radiating from Finn. Why did he act so snarly when all of this was hiding beneath the surface?

"Mommy would say yes," Lola responded, full of confidence.

"She lets us do lots of stuff," Sage added, always the first of the girls to push the boundaries on anything physical.

Reese stayed silent, letting her more outgoing sisters plead their case.

Ivy's cheeks creased. Man, she loved them. Their tenacity. Their big hearts residing inside of their little bodies.

"Mommy *would* say yes." Ivy approached them, and the girls broke out in a chorus of excitement, showing her the chicks, explaining what they were doing.

Once the hubbub ebbed, Finn's blueberry eyes held hers, an apology written in them. "Sorry I didn't check with you first. They came on the truck, the girls heard them chirping and the rest is history."

"They came in the mail?"

"Yep. They're brand-new, so the girls are helping me teach them how to eat and drink. The green stuff is high protein. It's supposed to help them recover from being shipped."

"I'd need something extra if I'd been shipped in a box, too." Ivy turned a bucket over next to the girls and copped a seat. "Who do I need to meet?"

"This one is Gracie and this one is Lala and this one is Bernadine." The girls pointed out their favorites.

"Those are really great names. And what did you name yours, Finn?"

His mouth bowed with humor and the warmth she knew existed inside of him. The warmth he kept snuffing out when he was around her.

"Fluffy." He lifted the chick to study it. "Definitely Fluffy."

Ivy's lips curved when his twinkling eyes met hers.

"That's a good name, Mista Finn," Lola declared.

"Thank you."

A call came from the barn entrance. "Sorry I'm late. I'm here. I'll get the truck loaded." The young man who'd appeared in the doorway disappeared just as quickly.

"That's Cliff. He's going to help me feed the cattle this afternoon."

"Can we go, too?" Sage asked. "We want to feed the cattles."

"Please, please," Lola and Reese joined in.

Finn's features softened at the girls' request, and Ivy's insides swirled. Maybe it was a good thing he was surly with them half the time. Because if he wasn't, she'd be in all-caps trouble.

"You can ride with me sometime, but not today. But I am going to need you girls to check on the chicks later today if you don't mind." He shot Ivy a questioning glance, asking her permission without words.

Yes, Finn Brightwood. You're letting us stay here for free. "Of course we'll check on the chicks. The girls would love nothing more." *And somehow, even though you doubt me, I'm going to prove that us being here is a help and not a hindrance.*

Ivy would figure out a way to earn their stay in the bunkhouse. Not because she thought everything in life had to be even steven, but because she was turning over a new leaf, and for her own mental health, she had to *know* that she wasn't mooching. That this was a two-way street.

And if she could prove that not only to herself but also to Finn…that would make her victory even sweeter.

Chapter Five

The gently used, highly rated espresso machine was a huge find. Ivy clicked to buy it, entering Charlie's credit card information on the laptop she'd stationed on the counter in the café. She couldn't wait to tell Charlie the low price.

Apparently the restaurant selling it had closed their doors and was trying to recoup some money from their assets. Ivy definitely didn't want Charlie's café following in those footsteps, but she was happy to take advantage of the reduced price. She crossed the machine off her list, then emailed the information to Charlie's accountant for bookkeeping purposes.

Shopping with someone else's money made Ivy nervous, but she and Charlie had discussed the costs for the various supplies needed. And Ivy had found the espresso machine quite a bit under budget, which was a win. Plus, the funds she was using weren't stolen, so Ivy wasn't committing a crime. Her stomach churned like the Atlantic during a nor'easter. Sometimes the guilt from what Lee had done reared up like a resounding slap in the face. How had she not known what he was up to? How could she have been that blind?

But I did know something *was up. I just didn't know what.*

Lee had made excellent money in the beginning of their marriage, so there'd been no blaring sirens to inform Ivy that his salary had taken a hit and he'd begun supplementing by dipping into pockets that weren't his.

Her phone played a few seconds of the girls' favorite song—her reminder it was time to pick them up.

Ms. Lina lived five minutes from the café in a small house that boasted a red door, blue siding and brightly colored flower boxes. Lina was just as artistic as her house, and the girls had benefited from the woman's creative side. Every day they came home with various art projects.

Ivy knocked and stepped inside when Lina called out a welcome. The Hispanic woman had her thick chocolate hair pulled back in a ponytail and wore a colorful, loose-fitting dress and multicolored glasses. She had grandkids who lived out of state, and their pictures dotted her walls and shelves. She'd told Ivy that her husband had passed away ten years ago, and she'd never had the desire to remarry. Ivy had understood the sentiment, but for a different reason. Where Lina's marriage had been wonderful and her husband had been her partner in every way, Ivy's marriage had been lacking in so many things—companionship, communication, trust.

The girls were huddled around the coffee table, painting pictures. They wore oversize button-up shirts over their clothes, and they were concentrating so hard they didn't notice her arrival.

"Hi, loves." She knelt beside them and was quickly tackled by three strong hugs.

The next two minutes were filled with descriptions of their day—what they'd played and eaten and how much fun they'd had. After a short checkup with Lina over how the time had really gone, Ivy wrangled the three of them into the Suburban. She'd thought they might nod off on the drive home—Lina had said no one had napped today—but they all managed to stay awake, filling every moment with anecdotes.

"Mommy, are we going to Ms. Lina's again tomorrow? Or are we going to Nana and Pop-pop's in California?" A glance in the rearview mirror confirmed Reese had asked the question while staring out the window, her little mind in overdrive as usual. "She said she has something fun planned for tomorrow." The wistfulness in her voice created an ache under Ivy's ribs.

"Yes, you're all going back to Ms. Lina's tomorrow. We're not going to Nana and Pop-pop's house until the second week in May, and there are a lot of days between now and then. Which means lots more art and playing. Okay?"

Reese nodded, her concerns momentarily abated.

The girls had suffered after their father's demise. While they didn't know the details of what had happened— though someday Ivy would have the painful privilege of explaining it to them—they understood their father's death and absence and the strange twist their life had taken. Their friends, gone. Their home, gone. Everything they'd known, gone.

Ivy was incredibly grateful that they were enjoying their time at Lina's so much. It appeased the doubts that had surfaced when Ivy had communicated the change in plans to her parents. The delay had not been well received by them. They'd adamantly argued with her decision to stay in Westbend, however temporary it was. And they most definitely didn't understand her reasons for opening the café for Charlie. And why would they? They had plenty of money and were all set to rescue Ivy and their granddaughters. And while Ivy appreciated the safety net, she wasn't ready to jump into it quite yet. She'd asked her parents to be patient with her even if they didn't agree with her choice.

At that, Dad had grunted and removed himself from the conversation. Her mom had spent the next five minutes ignoring everything Ivy had said, continuing to plead with her to *be logical* and *think of the girls*.

As if Ivy thought of anyone else.

Despite their doubts, Ivy felt like she *was* being logical. The reference from Charlie plus the experience she was gaining plus the chance to prove to herself that she was capable of taking care of her girls on her own... she needed all of it. Even if it was only short-term.

They pulled into the ranch drive, and a strange sense of home settled around Ivy. Maybe that was a gift from God after the reminder of the disquieting conversation with her parents.

The next two hours were spent making dinner— grilled cheese sandwiches on the hot plate Charlie had loaned to her—cuddling with the girls, hearing more about their day, playing games and deciding on outfits and breakfast for tomorrow. Planning ahead was the only way Ivy was juggling her new schedule. She'd never worked full-time after the girls' births, and it was an adjustment for all of them, but the triplets were rising to the challenge.

The four of them were emotionally and physically closer in the cozy bunkhouse than they'd ever been in their large, rambling house with the playroom and the professionally designed treehouse in the perfectly landscaped backyard.

At the ranch, the girls played outside and made up games purely from imagination. They were more creative here than they had been with everything they could have ever wanted at their fingertips back in Connecticut.

By seven o'clock, the girls were done. No naps along with the adjustment of going to Lina's each day had the three of them heading straight to meltdown town. Lola's propensity to be bossy was at its highest levels, Reese was whimpering over *everything* and Sage suggested to her sisters that they should climb up to the top bunk and take turns jumping down onto pillows.

Ivy directed everyone to don pajamas and brush their teeth, then settled them in the bunks. Sage and Reese were sharing the bottom bunk tonight, because Ivy had put a stop to one of the girls sleeping on the floor. That way she could sneak in to check on them at night without disturbing whoever was on the floor, and they weren't squirreling around climbing in and out of each other's beds.

Whichever girl was "first" for the day got the top bunk to themselves.

Ivy had implemented the rotating system when the girls had grown old enough to argue over who got to go first for *everything*.

Each day one of the girls was first, second or third, and they rotated through the order so that everyone was "first" on a revolving schedule. It avoided silly fights.

All she had to do was ask whose day it was, and the girls would fall into line, sometimes begrudgingly, but since they didn't want anyone to mess with their "first" day, no one bucked the system.

Ivy played a bedtime story on the girls' tablet, and the three of them all dropped off in ten minutes. Astounding.

Ms. Lina deserved an award for not only wrangling the girls all day but exhausting them to the point that they went to sleep easily.

Ivy entered the bedroom and winced at the bag of clothes that had fallen into the dirt when she'd been moving things inside the bunkhouse. She'd placed it on the bed this morning so that she'd remember to do laundry tonight. Most of the muddy items were for cold weather, and the sky was spitting snow yet again. With what the girls had already worn, they were running low on outfits. She could no longer avoid the need to do laundry…or the man who owned the house with the laundry set in it.

She'd talked herself out of attempting the Laundromat in town with the girls because she valued her sanity.

She sent a text to Finn.

I'm sorry to bug you, but would you mind if I did a couple loads of laundry?

She changed into yoga pants, tennis shoes and a comfortable sweatshirt, then gathered everything that needed to be washed as she waited for his answer. Ten minutes later, she had it.

Go ahead. I'm not at the house anyway.

Ivy made sure the video monitor that connected to the app on her phone was working before sneaking out the front door of the bunkhouse and locking it behind her. The wind whipped cold moisture under the collar of her jacket and down her spine as she stood outside and confirmed on the app screen that none of the girls had moved or woken.

Leaning into the bursts of wind, she made her way to Finn's house. The ranch truck with an attached trailer cut through the snowy night and came to a halt near the barn. Finn jumped out and ran around to the back of the trailer. Ivy's view of what he was removing from it was blocked, but Finn's haste was palpable.

Her feet switched directions without her permission. She found Finn in the barn, hurriedly scrubbing down a calf with a towel while others stood by. She dropped her bag of clothing in the corner and approached him.

"What's wrong? What's going on?" Were they sick? What was happening?

Finn jerked back in surprise, obviously having no idea of her presence. "Nothing yet. The weather turned and the calves are too young to survive the cold and wet. I'm just moving them inside."

"By yourself?"

Finn finished his ministrations and stood. "Yes. Both of my hands are off tonight. I was hoping the weather wouldn't be bad enough to warrant this, but the drop in temperature along with the moisture is too much."

"I'll help."

At Ivy's declaration, his brow furrowed. "Where are the girls?"

"Asleep." She fumbled to remove her phone from

her pocket and showed him the video of them. No one had so much as rolled over from their original position.

He considered the screen. "What if one of them wakes up? I'll handle this. The girls need you."

He moved on to the next calf, and Ivy grew bold. She stepped next to him and stole the towel from his hand. "If anything happens, I can easily check on them. It's only a few yards from here. And I locked the door. They can't wander outside or anything."

"I still don't think it's a good idea."

"You don't have a choice." Ivy mimicked Finn's movements on the next calf. After about thirty seconds of silence, he gave in and left the barn. The truck engine roared to life, and Ivy's shoulders dropped as air rushed from her lungs. "Sometimes you just have to stand your ground, am I right?" The calf she'd rubbed down bellowed in answer.

Ivy continued the one-sided conversation, hoping the sound of her voice was soothing to the animals and not alarming. "You're going to be just fine. And so are your...siblings or cousins or whatever you cattle refer to each other as. Finn's going to make sure you're all safe, okay?"

And even though she'd only known the man for a little over two weeks, Ivy was strangely confident he'd do exactly that.

And strangely victorious that she would be there to help him accomplish it.

With the last few calves loaded, Finn made his final retreat to the barn. Each time he'd returned, Ivy had been there, working continuously to bring the animals back from their frozen state. He'd shown her the supplemental feed, and she'd also begun bottle-feeding them per his directions.

He unloaded the calves.

"Keep them separate." Ivy directed him with a wave of her hand. "This group's been fed."

Finn's jaw loosened as he followed her order. Not all of the calves had been fed, but more than he'd expected. How had she gotten so much done in the time he'd been gone?

He joined Ivy with another bottle and worked through the remaining cattle. Between the hay, the shared warmth from the calves and the heat lamp, the barn was toasty enough for the animals to survive the night, but Finn would still get up in a few hours to check on them.

"How are the girls doing?" Finn didn't like that they were in the bunkhouse unattended, but Ivy was the parent, not him.

"They're doing great. I went back to the bunkhouse while you were gone. No one's moved. Ms. Lina must have had them run a couple of miles today."

His mouth curved to match hers.

"How come you didn't have to do this during the other snowstorm? The night the girls and I slid off the road?"

"Because the calves weren't born yet. They started dropping after that."

"Ah. I see."

Finn switched from feeding one calf to another. "Gage Frasier—I'm not sure if you've met him at church. He's married to Emma. She's one of the Wilder siblings who run Wilder Guest Ranch. I used to work there back in the day. That's how I ended up deciding I wanted to settle near Westbend. Anyway, Gage inherited his uncle's ranch a couple years back, and he switched to summer calving. Says it prevents issues like this and has increased his profitability. I need to talk to him about it sometime." Finn wouldn't mind *not* spending his spring chasing calves, attempting to save them from freezing temps or snowstorms that could take them under.

"Would I have met him at the cattlemen's dinner?"

"No. Emma's sister, Mackenzie, was pregnant and went into labor that day, so they were with family. Mackenzie's husband is Jace Hawke. Evan Hawke's brother. Evan is married to Addie, Charlie's good friend."

Ivy stared at him. "I have no idea what you just said."

He laughed. "Me, either. Suffice to say, you can play Six Degrees with pretty much everyone in Westbend and find a connection."

When they finished feeding the last batch, Ivy straightened and placed a hand on her lower back. Not used to this kind of work, no doubt. Not that it had showed tonight. She'd hung in with the best of them.

"I'm guessing you didn't get your laundry done."

The bag was still in the corner of the barn where she'd first dropped it. "Nope. That's okay. The girls can re-wear some of the things without stains. We'll be fine."

"Speaking of the girls…you should check on them. I'll bring you something to warm you up. It's hard to get the chill out of your bones on a night like tonight."

"Oh, you don't have to do that. I'll be fine."

"You don't have a choice."

Ivy's smile blossomed when he repeated the phrase

she'd said earlier, and he ignored the way his heart hitched in response.

"Okay. I'm going to shower when I get back to the bunkhouse. Due to all of the calves'—" she paused as if searching for the right word "—bodily functions that I've encountered tonight. I might have to burn this clothing, which is disappointing, since these are my favorite yoga pants."

"We'll get them clean. Don't light the match just yet. Can you handle coffee at this time of night?"

"Yep. I'll still sleep like a baby. Especially after all of that."

"Okay good. I'll see you in twenty then." The last thing Finn needed was to worry about Ivy catching a cold because she'd been helping him out. He'd make sure she was good to go and then hit the sack himself for a few hours.

They leaned into the weather as they headed for their respective homes, Ivy toting the bag of laundry back to the bunkhouse with her. He would offer to throw a load in for her, but he figured both of them were too exhausted to deal with that tonight.

Finn started a pot of decaf, then showered and dressed in clean jeans, boots and a waffle-knit long-sleeved shirt. He poured the coffee into a thermos and tossed a package of Girl Scout cookies one of the munchkins at church had sold him into a bag. He then added a mug and some of the creamers Charlie had left at his house since he remembered Ivy using them. Maybe she had her own at the bunkhouse, maybe not.

He bundled up and walked over to Ivy's. She must have been watching for him, because the door opened before he could knock. Finn had planned to deliver the hot liquid and sugar, then depart, but Ivy pulled him inside.

"It's okay. They won't wake up."

The sound of ocean waves came from the girls' partially open door, and Ivy scooted across the space to close it fully. The two of them settled into the chairs that filled the small living room/would-be-kitchen. Finn retrieved the mug, coffee and cookies, placing them on the coffee table, and Ivy's eyes widened with pleasure at the last item.

"The mint ones are my favorites." After doctoring her coffee, she took two. "Aren't you going to have any coffee?"

"I...didn't grab two mugs."

She hopped up and came back with a paper coffee cup for him.

Ivy had her phone, app open, on the coffee table, and they both watched as one of the girls—Finn couldn't tell which from the black-and-white screen—rotated in her bed. After that, silence and no more fidgeting.

"Do they always sleep this well?"

"Once they're out, yes. Otherwise I would never have considered leaving them here while I was in the barn. But usually getting them down is much more of a marathon than it was tonight. They pretty much always manage to find some excuse to get out of bed, like needing a glass of water. Or needing to use the restroom. Or that one sister is making funny noises and bothering the other two. Or they come up with a million random stories or questions." She finished her second cookie. "The serving size on these should be one whole package."

Finn's mouth curved. He liked this relaxed, open version of Ivy. Maybe a little too much.

"What are you doing here, Ivy?" He cringed at his harsh inquiry. He hadn't meant to say something like that. The plan had been to thank her, not interrogate her.

Ivy didn't flinch, didn't act surprised. She blew on her coffee before taking a sip. "What do you actually want to know, Finn?"

She didn't beat around the bush. He respected that. Maybe even appreciated it. "I mean, besides my sister pushing you toward staying, because I know how she can be, how come you decided to open the café instead of just moving on to your parents'? Especially when that is your final plan."

"It is my final plan. I just… Ever since my marriage failed and the girls lost their dad and we lost…everything, I've known that I would have to start over at my parents' because I'm not qualified to do anything anymore. I haven't worked outside of a few hours at a clothing store in years. I've been a stay-at-home mom. Feels like I don't count out in the real world sometimes."

"That's not true. Being a stay-at-home mom takes incredible skill." His mom had done the same.

"Thank you. But try writing that on an application or a résumé. Opening the café for Charlie, with Charlie…it sounds like finding a piece of myself again. Like proving something to myself. Maybe even to my parents. She said she'd give me a reference for when we move on to California, and I could use that." She shrugged. "But that's my problem, Finn. Not yours. I didn't know Charlie was going to suggest me not paying rent. I'm sorry we were dumped on you. If you don't want us here, it's okay. You can say so."

Her deep lake-blue eyes were knowing as they met

his. Of course she'd been able to recognize his hissy fit the day she'd been moving items into the bunkhouse.

He'd been so worried about rescuing Ivy, but tonight, she'd rescued him. If he'd been on his own, he'd still be working. Still be locating calves and praying that he hadn't lost any in the weather.

Thanks to Ivy, that hadn't happened.

"I'm not asking you to leave."

"You're not asking us to stay, either."

"Can the one be enough?" Finn's pulse faltered, then revved. This was his opportunity to shirk out of having Ivy and the girls stay in the bunkhouse, but he couldn't take it. She needed this time in Westbend, and who was Finn to steal that from her? He wasn't rescuing her. She was rescuing herself, and all he had to do was stay out of her way. That wasn't breaking the rules he'd set for himself.

Ivy studied him, contemplative. Pretty. Even prettier now that he'd seen her heart on her sleeve while she'd worked alongside him tonight. "Maybe. I do need the place if I'm going to stay in Westbend with the girls. And the first week of work at the café has been great. It made me feel valuable and alive again. Not that the girls don't do that. They do. They're everything to me. But I want them to know the version of their mom who existed ten years ago. Before Lee. I used to be amazing. A strange thing to say, right? But I look back on that young woman, and I think, where did she go? What happened to her? I want her back. My girls need her. *I* need her. And I think staying here, having the opportunity to open the café for Charlie, will give me back a piece of her."

"I'm looking at that woman right now. I don't know

where you think she went, but everything you've done since you arrived here matches everything you just said about that old version of yourself."

He hadn't meant to travel down the road of encouraging Ivy. Not when that was how things had first begun with Chrissa. But after Ivy had helped him with the calves and opened up to him, Finn couldn't keep the assurance to himself.

"I wouldn't have accomplished what I did tonight without you. I'd still be out there. And who knows how much work I'd have left."

Ivy teared up slightly, then blinked, causing the moisture to scatter. "Thank you." The short gratitude seemed to encompass so much more. It was a thank-you for the words, yes, but also a thank-you for letting them stay, for letting her find herself again.

"You're welcome." Finn could only pray he wouldn't come to regret that he'd had a second opportunity to send Ivy away…and he hadn't used it.

Chapter Six

Brown leather ankle boots or red flats? Ivy analyzed her choices with one shoe on each foot. Her camel sweater belted at the waist, and her jeans were dark indigo. The red added a pop of color, but the boots were more practical in inclement weather. It hadn't snowed in the week and a half since she'd helped Finn with the calves, though, so the flats weren't an outrageous option.

She'd fit in one quick load of laundry the Saturday after their save-the-calves adventure, but Finn hadn't been home. Besides church last week—she hadn't spotted him at this morning's service—their interactions had been in passing. Which Ivy was fine with, of course.

Just fine.

She couldn't possibly *want* to see the man, could she?

Ivy found the girls impatiently waiting for her in the living room.

"What time is the party at, Mommy?" asked Reese. "Are we going to miss it?"

"No, we're not going to miss it. We'll be right on

time." Or perhaps a few minutes late. Ivy wasn't about to share that news with three little cherubs whose concept of time revolved around morning, bedtime, meals and snacks. "Help me decide which shoes to wear and then we'll go."

Lola pondered her mom's selections, her finger toggling back and forth. "Red ones."

Of course Lola would be the one to have an opinion. She cared about fashion, always coordinating her outfits perfectly and accessorizing with a bracelet or a necklace, even if they were plastic.

The other two shrugged with indifference. Back in her room, Ivy slipped off the ankle boot, slid on the flat, then grabbed her purse and keys, plus the small birthday gift she'd purchased for Charlie.

Charlie had only agreed to let her friend Addie throw her a birthday dinner if none of the guests brought gifts. Ivy was breaking that rule, but only by a smidgeon.

The dainty gold necklace with the simple circle pendant barely counted as a present. And Ivy hadn't been able to let the opportunity to thank and celebrate Charlie pass by without commemorating it. Being around confident Charlie was good for Ivy. The woman trusted her to make decisions but was there when she needed someone to bounce an idea off. They'd accomplished so much at the café in the last two and a half weeks. And Ivy had learned so much from observing Charlie. Whatever Ivy did next, she'd be a better version of herself because of her temporary boss.

"At the birthday party, Ms. Charlie will get gifts, but we won't." Lola coached her sisters as they climbed into the Suburban. "We can't throw a fit about it."

"That is true. Definitely no fits." Ivy scanned for

Finn or his truck before leaving the ranch but found neither. She'd thought they might drive together if the timing worked, but the man was obviously off doing something.

He would be at the party, though, right? Of course he would. Finn and Charlie were close. He wouldn't miss his sister's birthday dinner.

And why do I care so much?

Ivy hadn't conversed with him much since the snowstorm, so she was simply curious as to how he was and how the calves had fared. That was all.

She pulled up directions to Little Red Hen Bed & Breakfast on her phone and started the drive into town. Ivy was excited to check out the B & B and have something social with adult conversation on her calendar. Addie was hosting them on a Sunday afternoon because her guests had checked out this morning and she didn't have more due until Thursday.

"Will there be balloons at the party, Mommy?" Sage was no doubt wondering what sort of game—or trouble—she could use them for if yes.

"I don't know. Possibly."

"There will be cake, right? Nobody has a birthday party without cake." Lola's tone was equal parts concerned and confident.

"If not cake, then I imagine there will be some sort of dessert."

A collective cheer came from the back seat.

"Who will we play with, Mommy?" Sweet Reese with her concern.

"There will be a little girl named Honor who's five." Charlie had fostered Honor last fall and she was Ryker's niece. She'd mentioned that Honor's mom sometimes worked weekends, so she and Ryker would have Honor with them. "And Ms. Addie has a little boy named Sawyer. He's three, like you girls." Ivy had met Addie and Sawyer when they'd stopped by the café to see Charlie on Tuesday, and she'd instantly liked the woman. "There might be a few other kids, too. I'm not sure."

The idea of new people must have ignited Reese's apprehension, because in the rearview mirror, Ivy spotted tears sliding down her cheeks.

Lola took her hand on one side. Sage did the same on the other.

Ivy loved that they always had each other's backs, even when they were opposite personalities on so many things.

"If it doesn't work to play with anyone else you always have each other. Built-in sister-friends."

Once she parked, they piled out of the vehicle, and Ivy's stomach squeezed with a flash of that panic Reese had experienced in the car. She needed adult conversation, and yet, showing up alone without a partner—to parties or in life—still shocked her at times. Lee had been gone for over a year, and somehow she could still be angry with him and miss having a person at the same time.

Not that he'd ever been her biggest supporter. But he'd never been cruel, either. Never abused her. He'd simply been distant. As if their worlds had been parallel and not in sync. Ivy had grieved more for the girls when he'd taken his life than she had for herself, since their relationship had never been what she'd hoped and imagined it would be.

She knocked on the front door, and Charlie welcomed her inside. "Come in. Girls, the kids are out back playing. I'll walk you out there so you can see what they're up to and if you want to join them." Charlie's contagious smile switched to Ivy. "And then I'll introduce you to everyone."

"Great." Her response was heavy with equal parts apprehension and acceptance.

Ivy admired the B & B's beautiful wood floors and original architecture as they headed for the back door.

Since the surprise snowstorm, the weather had warmed, though the girls wore sweatshirts to combat the remaining chill in the air.

"This is Honor." Charlie placed her hand on a little girl's head after they stepped outside. She was only slightly bigger in size than the triplets, but her curls were the stuff of legends. "Honor, can you show these girls how to play whatever it is you're all playing?"

"Sure!"

Charlie introduced each of the triplets. Reese dropped her gaze. Sage's fingers slipped into her mouth as intrigue ignited in her blue depths.

Lola piped up quickly, "We'll play, but I can't do anything to ruin my shoes." She twisted her leg to show off her navy ankle boots with side fringe.

Addie came out of the house, her son, Sawyer, bounding behind her.

She greeted Ivy and the girls. "Sawyer wants to play, too." She gently snagged the boy's arm, effectively holding him captive for her next statement. "All you kiddos need to stay between the cottage and the B & B, okay? We don't need anyone wandering into the forest and getting lost."

After the kids collectively acknowledged Addie's admonition, Honor motioned to the triplets. "Come on.

We'll start a new game." She, Sawyer and the girls all entered the fray with the other children.

A golden retriever loped up to Ivy and sniffed her knees.

"That's Belay," Addie explained, her concerned gaze still focused on Sawyer. "She was Evan's dog, but now I'd say she's more Sawyer's."

Belay settled by Addie's feet, observing the children like a protective, doting grandparent, and the woman bent to rub the dog's ears. "You're a good help, aren't you, Belay?" Addie straightened, directing her attention to Ivy. "Sawyer's a bit of an escape artist. He's been better lately, but he still makes me nervous."

"I can stay out here and watch the kids," Charlie offered.

"No need. I'll take a shift." Evan Hawke came down the back steps, the prosthesis Charlie had mentioned him having almost fully hidden by his pants. Addie had introduced Ivy to her husband at church this morning, and even in that short window, Ivy had witnessed his quiet, steady devotion to Addie and Sawyer. "It's too people-y for me in there anyway." Evan squeezed Charlie's shoulder. "And the birthday girl should really be inside with the other adults. Ryker was just looking for you."

Addie wrapped her arms around her husband's torso and squeezed. "How did you know I'd feel better with an adult out here keeping tabs on the kids? Sawyer in particular."

Evan pressed a kiss to the top of Addie's hair. "I know you. I've got you."

The simplicity of their love and connection... Ivy barely held back a sniffle.

The three women made their way inside. Ivy met the other couples from church—parents to the other kids outside—and then she and Charlie pitched in with the rest of the dinner preparations.

Addie had made numerous pans of lasagna—wa-sagna in triplet-speak—plus salad and bread. The house brimmed with the scents of garlic and oregano and everything good and homey.

Conversation flowed easily as they set out the food, paper plates, disposable tableware and napkins. Ivy's momentary panic from when she'd first arrived faded quickly. Never would she have thought that sliding off the road could bring so much good into her life. Addie and Charlie reminded her of her college roommates. She'd had the best girlfriends before Lee. But after her relationship with him had started, Ivy had slowly but surely lost touch with all of her friends. Her desperation to please Lee and make her marriage successful had overtaken all of her efforts and attention.

"We should feed the kids first." Addie paused to survey everything when it was ready. "That way they can go back out to play after, and the adults can enjoy their meals without getting up fifty times."

"Sounds perfect to me," Ivy agreed.

They called the kids in from the back and had them wash up. Ivy helped the girls through the line and situated them at the round table surrounded by a bench near the front windows that Addie referred to as the breakfast nook. The girls ate generous portions of wa-sagna, plenty of bread and small amounts of salad—a requirement of Ivy's they often attempted to avoid.

The kids around the table talked over each other

as they slurped down cups of lemonade and discussed what to play next.

Ivy's heart expanded like a balloon filling her chest. It was good to see the girls so relaxed and happy. Reese had even set aside her concerns for the afternoon. She didn't say as much as her sisters, but she listened with interest to the conversation going on around her.

Finn arrived just as the kids finished eating and the adults were forming a line. He greeted everyone with ease, hugging and teasing Charlie, man-hugging Ryker and Evan.

His mannerisms were like a crime TV show that Ivy couldn't stop binge-watching. How could he be so personable and yet have been so guarded with her at first? After she'd helped him with the calves, Finn had taken care of her by bringing over cookies and coffee. No matter how much he tried to hide who he really was, it always seeped through. Ivy wished she had asked him during their conversation what it was that he was burying. Especially since he'd asked her straight out why she was staying in town.

At least while helping with the calves she'd accomplished her goal of proving that she wasn't freeloading and that she could be as much of a help to Finn as he was to her. The way he'd thanked her for her assistance and confessed how much longer things would have taken without her had given Ivy a huge lift. She'd barely resisted letting out a victory whoop.

Ivy took a plate and filtered through the food line.

Finn ended up next to her.

"I haven't seen much of you since the snowstorm. I mean, I've seen you running, but that's about it," she said.

Finn's shoulders lifted along with his mouth. "Calving season is the busiest. I have been running."

"Let me know if you need any more of my expert ranching help."

The skin around his eyes crinkled. "I'll do that. How've you been?" He seemed genuine, so Ivy gave him genuine.

"The girls appear to be adjusting to their new normal. Although, this morning in Sunday school, Lina told me they got into trouble."

"How'd they manage that?"

"They told everyone that Lina was theirs. As in *their* possession. And that she loved them more than she loved the other kids in the class."

Finn laughed. "What did Lina do?"

"She'd taken care of it by the time I arrived to pick them up. I believe a time-out and apologies were in order."

"And what about you, outside of the girls?" Finn scooped salad onto his plate.

The question surprised her. Sometimes Ivy forgot there was a *her* outside of the girls. "I'm enjoying working with your sister so much." She plated a piece of lasagna and inhaled the scent. What she wouldn't give to have the time and the kitchen to make her homemade lasagna. She loved to cook and used it as a creative outlet and stress reliever. But between moving, the accident and now working full-time and living in the unfinished bunkhouse, she hadn't had the opportunity in ages. "Charlie's fantastic. I feel like I'm learning a lot from her about making decisions and trusting my instincts."

"That's great news. I'm glad. Just don't tell her that. Don't need her to get a big head."

Amused by their playful exchange, Ivy grabbed a set of the plastic cutlery from the end of the island. "How have things been with the ranch?"

"I lost a calf to a coyote the other day, so I've been checking the herd constantly. Cliff and Behr have been working extra. I should really hire someone else, but I can't decide if it will stay this busy or if things will even out once the calves age."

"Or if you should just wear yourself to the bone handling everything on your own."

"Exactly." He chuckled and followed her into the dining room.

Ivy took the corner spot and Finn sat at the end of the table next to her. After three bites, her phone vibrated in her pocket, and she checked the screen. Her mom. If she didn't answer, the woman would call back numerous times until she did.

"I'd better take this. Excuse me a second."

Ivy moved into the living room that lined the front of the house and swiped to answer, her stomach dropping to the soles of her red flats. She wanted to stay at the dining table with Finn and the others, but if she didn't deal with her mom, it would put a dark cloud over the rest of her evening.

Hopefully, the conversation she was about to engage in wouldn't do the same.

Ivy's food grew cold as the talk around Finn bounced from one topic to another. Ryker left the table and returned a minute later with an extra piece of bread for Charlie. For a second, Finn had wondered if he was leaving to grab a ring and coming back in to propose. He and Charlie had certainly talked about marriage plenty. They were obviously heading in that direction. Finn was starting to wonder what Ryker was waiting for, especially since the man's feelings for Charlie were as obvious as the tattoo scrawled across his forearm.

"Is Ivy still on the phone?" Charlie quietly checked with Ryker, who nodded.

"Pretty sure it was her mom who called." Finn was sitting close enough to Ryker and Charlie that he could join their conversation without raising curiosity. "I saw the screen when she checked it."

His sister's brow wrinkled. "I hope everything is okay."

He did, too. When Finn had spoken to Ivy while getting food, it had felt comfortable and easy. Like old friends catching up. It had once again laid his rescuing fears to rest. Especially when Ivy had shared how much she was enjoying working with Charlie. But when she'd cringed at her mom's call and then answered anyway, his protective instincts had flared.

Was she okay? *Was* something wrong? Should he check on her or stay out of it?

Door number two, Brightwood. Definitely door number two. Stick to your original plan.

"I'm going to grab seconds. Anyone need anything?" After a chorus of noes, he walked through the living room on his way back to the kitchen.

Ivy was in the chair in the corner of the room, her head held in her hands, the phone pressed against her ear.

Finn's feet betrayed him and came to a screeching halt. The temptation to stride over to her, rip the phone from her grip and end the call—or toss it out the window—was staggering.

"Mom, the girls are doing well. Staying here for a short amount of time isn't going to harm them."

If anything, it might be good for the girls. Having someone like Lina care for them certainly had its pluses.

"I'm sorry you thought I'd change my mind, but that's not the case. And I'm certainly not leaving Charlie in the lurch like that." A pause ensued before Ivy continued. "Mom, I've told you this numerous times. Charlie is the woman who owns the café I'm helping open."

Finn forced his boots to move. Enough eavesdropping. Ivy would be fine.

She glanced up and saw him just as he neared the large opening that led back to the kitchen. Her free hand waved and signaled for him to stop. He'd just been listening to her conversation like a buffoon. She was probably going to yank on his ear and tell him to mind his own business.

"Mom—Mom, listen! Someone is here and needs me. I have to go. I'll talk to you soon, okay? Try not to worry."

She hung up, an agitated breath seeping from her.

"Sorry. I didn't mean to overhear or interrupt."

She stood and pocketed the phone. "I'm glad you walked through right then. You were just the excuse I needed to hang up. I don't know how many times I can say the same thing. I know she's just concerned about the girls and me, but man, she makes it hard."

"It's a mom thing. If I don't call mine often enough, I start getting texts asking if I'm alive." Finn's mouth quirked. He did love his mother. And compared to Ivy's mom, she was incredibly easy. "Was she like this when you were married?"

"No. Not really. Because then I had my life together. Or so they thought. Lee made good money before he made mistakes. I think my parents checked off a box after I married him. My dad may not have agreed or liked Lee in the first place, but at least I was on my own and functioning. They weren't having to take care of me like some of their friends were with their grown children." Ivy's lids momentarily closed as if she was in pain. "And now, here I am in that same boat. Is it any wonder I'm not in a rush to go home? I felt like a failure when Lee stole. When Lee took his life and left the girls. And now going back to live with my parents is like the cherry on top of a terrible, messed-up sundae."

"Everyone is allowed a few mistakes in life, Ivy. So you thought you chose well in marriage but it didn't turn out that way. That happens to a lot of people. Not just you."

"Feels like it's just me."

Tell her. Tell her about Chrissa so that she doesn't think she's the only one who thought they knew what they were doing but found out they were dead wrong.

"Listen—" Footsteps sounded behind Finn. He glanced back to see one of the women from church walking toward the kitchen. He waited for her to pass, and his original words fled. "You're going to be okay. You're doing a good job with what you've been handed." The encouragement was a pale substitution.

"Thanks." Her sigh was as long as a summer day. "The last time I stood up to them, I married Lee. I don't think anyone trusts my judgment anymore, including myself." She attempted a laugh, to bring humor into something that was obviously hurtful to her. It didn't work. "Has anyone sung happy birthday to Charlie yet?"

"No. At least I don't think so. But we can make that happen if you need to go." Finn warred between regret over not opening up to Ivy and relief that his own failures and hurts were still buried deep.

Her mom's phone call had only served to remind him—and Ivy, he would guess—of the mess she was running from. And to, it seemed. She had a lot to work through and three girls who needed her to do it well.

All things he should stay out of.

"It's not that. I'm not leaving yet. The girls would throw fits if I tried to remove them early from the world's best playdate. I could just really use a piece of cake."

Finn's cheeks creased, and he ignored the way his heart kicked and jumped over the revelation that she wasn't running.

"We can definitely make that happen."

"What flavor is it anyway?"

"I'm guessing chocolate. That's Charlie's favorite."

Ivy's smile was warm and pretty and unable to completely mask her distress. "God bless Charlie."

Chapter Seven

Ivy waited for her fourth interview of the day to walk into the café, nerves souring her stomach as if she'd downed a cup of vinegar. Talking to people didn't bother her. Finding out who they were, what interested them, what drove them…that was all part of getting to know someone.

But being in charge of hiring for the café was so much more than that. Ivy might like an applicant and think they were a fit, but what if they turned out not to be? What if they didn't show up on time, or their declared customer service skills were sorely lacking?

Since Ivy would be moving to California shortly after the opening, Charlie should really be handling these interviews. She was the one who'd have to work closely with the staff and new manager. But Charlie didn't have the time…and on this next interview, she wanted to stay as uninvolved as possible.

The door opened, and an attractive young woman entered the café. She wore a striped suit that was a size too large, and her hand shook when she ran it through her curly dark-roast hair.

Kaia. Ryker's sister.

Ivy could definitely see the resemblance between her and her daughter, Honor.

Even in their short greeting, brokenness poured from Kaia. Charlie had filled Ivy in on Kaia's background. She'd been through a lot, fighting a drug addiction that had caused her to lose Honor for a period. Despite her brave, shaky smile, the wounds from her past showed.

"I'm nervous." Kaia wiped her palms down the front of her pants as they sat at one of the round tables that would soon be used for patrons. "Asking for an interview was hard because I didn't want to bug Charlie for another favor. She's already done so much for Honor. She was Honor's foster parent—I assume she told you?"

"She did."

"I don't want to take advantage of our relationship or the fact that she's dating my brother, but the thought of working here—" her eyes bounced around the café with interest and light and something close to hope "—was more than I could pass up. I'm glad my interview is with you. That way we can be brutally honest with each other."

Did they have to?

Ivy understood that Charlie had taken herself out of the equation because she was too emotionally invested in Honor and Ryker and even Kaia, but it was stressful to think she was somehow responsible for deciding if Kaia was a fit for the job or not.

"So what do you do for work right now, Kaia?"

"I clean businesses and houses. It's good work, and I'm thankful for it. Especially after...everything. They gave me a second chance. Seems like I've been needing a lot of those lately."

Haven't we all? "I've heard really great things about you from Charlie and your brother."

"Both of them have been so supportive of Honor and me. That's why asking for an interview to work at the café was so hard. I know I'm not qualified to work here. I'm not really qualified to do anything but clean. That's all I've ever done. But I want to push myself, if not for me, then for my daughter. I'd do anything for her."

"I have three girls, so I completely understand that sentiment." *And I get the unqualified feeling, big-time.*

"Tell me more about you," Ivy said.

"After battling an addiction to meth, I've basically only focused on work and Honor and staying on the straight and narrow. A guy really messed with me." Kaia held up a palm. "Not that I'm making excuses for my actions. It was still my choice to do what I did. But I got off track and getting back on took every last ounce of me."

Everything Kaia was saying resonated with Ivy. Their stories might have different pieces filling in the puzzle, but they had plenty of similarities.

"What do you like and dislike about your current job?"

"It's great in that it pays the bills, and the work is consistent. But it's just not my passion."

"What is your passion?"

"Would it be bad to admit that I'm not sure yet? I'm twenty-four and feel like I'm still figuring that out. But the café appeals to me because I'd love to work directly with people. When I'm cleaning, I'm usually on my own or with one other person. We don't have much interaction with the customer, and I think I'd really like that."

She'd definitely get that at the café. "What about

hours? Charlie is planning to be open until four, but there might be some evening hours, too." Ivy had pitched Charlie an idea she'd had about allowing local groups and committees to use the café space after hours for meetings. It would require a staff member to take a later shift, but the event side could be a nice addition to the bottom line. Charlie had agreed that Ivy should follow up on the idea when she had time.

"I can make that work. Maybe not every day, but if I know my schedule, my brother is usually willing to help out with Honor."

That had been another one of Ivy's questions—whether Kaia had childcare when Honor wasn't in school.

They went on to discuss what Kaia's strengths and weaknesses were. She was far too hard on herself, quickly mentioning the areas in which she struggled and then scrounging to find good things to say. Ivy related to that, too. Kaia was a younger version of Ivy except she'd grown up with less money and less help.

It made Ivy want to give the woman a chance. Maybe too much.

They wrapped up the interview with Ivy promising to let Kaia know either way.

Ivy grabbed the girls from Lina's, and they began bickering over something pointless in the back seat before she'd even made it out of the driveway. Normally she would put a stop to it, but her brain was fried from the day and the endless processing of the four candidates. She didn't have enough energy to referee.

What she wouldn't give to release some of the stress from today in a kitchen…only she didn't have one of those.

Finn did, though.

He'd offered her his kitchen and laundry facilities before. If he hadn't meant it, he shouldn't have said it.

Ivy pulled into the lot for Len's Grocery, freed the girls from their car seats and managed to grab the ingredients for chicken scampi with angel-hair pasta—a favorite meal of hers—without completely losing her mind.

Unsure of her plan, she drove home. Should she text Finn and ask? Or just show up at his door with groceries in hand?

Ivy wasn't oblivious to the fact that Charlie had paved the way for their stay in the bunkhouse and that Finn's secondary agreement had been reluctant. He'd never complained outright about them being there, though she often wondered what he was thinking or the basis behind his quiet concern.

At the birthday party, he'd been kind and supportive after her phone call with her mom, but that didn't mean he was letting her into his life in any way. Finn Brightwood definitely had some walls up. What Ivy wouldn't give to know the secrets that were propping them in place.

She pulled into the ranch drive. Finn's truck was gone, and no lights were on in his house. How great was that? She'd shoot him a text about using the laundry and kitchen, but maybe she and the girls would be out of his space before he returned home. He'd told her he kept a key under the flowerpot on the front step.

"We're going to go over to Finn's house tonight to cook dinner and do laundry." They were majorly overdue on clean clothes.

"Will Mista Finn be home?"

"No," she answered Lola.

"But what will we do there?" Reese's inquiry was an eight on the whining scale.

"You girls could watch a movie while I make dinner." Ms. Lina was great about allowing them very little electronic time during the day. Letting the girls watch something would allow Ivy to relax while cooking.

All three cheered, then began arguing over what to watch. Ivy rolled her eyes and laughed.

She wouldn't make it one day without her babies. But she wouldn't mind five minutes to unwind from her day…in peace.

Finn's headlights beamed through the first signs of dusk as he left the Blairs' house in town and drove home.

Jacob Blair attended the same early-morning men's Bible study as Finn, and his son had a rare disease—autoimmune encephalitis. The family was so taxed that Jacob didn't have time to tackle any projects around the house, so a group of men from study—Finn, Ryker, Evan, Evan's brother, Jace, and Jace's brothers-in-law, Luc Wilder and Gage Frasier—had decided to spend the evening checking off items and fixing things that needed repair.

The six of them had fixed the washer, adjusted a broken front step and installed shelving in the garage so that the Blairs could organize and make room for parking both of their vehicles. It had been equal parts enjoyable—Finn liked everyone who'd pitched in—and equal parts painful.

Because witnessing Ryan Blair reeling from his last treatment had leveled Finn.

He didn't know how Jacob and Jenny handled seeing their son in pain day after day. He didn't know how any parent handled witnessing their child's suffering. Certainly, it was because there was no other choice but *to* handle it. With God.

Somehow.

When he pulled into the ranch drive, his house was lit up like Westbend's favorite ice-cream shop after a big game. Through the windows, he could see the TV was on, and he caught a glimpse of Ivy in the kitchen.

He would imagine she'd texted him, but he hadn't checked his phone while at the Blairs' or before leaving.

He would also have imagined that returning home to find his house taken over by four Darlings would overwhelm or upset him.

But he only felt relief.

The scene when he opened the front door was something out of another man's life.

The triplets were sprawled in various places in the living room, watching something on the TV, and the stove held a dish that simmered and smelled amazing.

Ivy came down the hall with a basket of laundry. She set it on the floor next to the island, straightened and noticed him.

"Oh." Her eyes widened, and her palm slapped to her sternum as if he'd shocked her.

Finn removed his jacket, hanging it in the hall closet. "You really have to stop breaking and entering."

Ivy laughed. "I'm working on it. Did you get my text?"

"No, I didn't see it." His theory that she would have notified him was spot-on. Ivy wasn't the kind to barge in without announcing herself. She wasn't the kind to barge in at all. She'd been very careful to give him space, which he appreciated. Tonight, he appreciated the opposite.

Nothing could take his mind off the tough scene at the Blairs' better than these four.

The girls flocked in his direction with cries of *Mista Finn*. Sage catapulted herself over the back of the couch instead of going around like her sisters, which earned a squeak of indignation from Ivy.

"Sage Renee Darling. You know better than that. Don't treat Finn's house that way again. You owe him an apology."

Sage was the first to hug Finn since she'd taken a shortcut, and her mischievous eyes twinkled as he knelt, and she crashed into him.

"Sorry, Mista Finn." She spoke around the fingers that had sneaked into her mouth.

"It's okay. I forgive you." His vision met Ivy's over the girl's shoulder. "Besides, it's just furniture."

"Mista Finn! Mista Finn!" Lola and Reese whapped into him at the same time, sandwiching their sister in the process.

Finn fought back the emotion today had created, focusing instead on the triple hug. He wanted to tell them they could call him Finn, but he wasn't sure if Ivy would approve of that. Besides, the *mista* amused and entertained him.

When the girls released their holds and stepped back, Reese shyly studied the floor. "I maded you something today at Ms. Lina's."

His heart turned to mush. "That's the sweetest thing I've heard all day. Can I see it?"

"It's not here. Mommy said you wouldn't be here."

"Is it at the bunkhouse?"

Her head bobbed.

"Maybe we can grab it in a bit, okay?"

Reese beamed like he'd promised her a trip to Disney World.

He wanted to hug each of the girls again and whisper in their ears to live long and well and to never get sick, but he cut himself off from doing that. No one could dictate the future, no matter how much Finn craved that very thing.

The triplets returned to their movie, and like a magnet, his feet led him to Ivy in the kitchen.

"So you came home to all of this without warning." Her waving hand encompassed the living room and kitchen. "That's terrible. I'm so sorry, Finn. We've taken over your house and you didn't even know to expect it. We'll get out of here. I can pack this up." She pointed to the dinner with the spatula in her hand. "We can eat at the bunkhouse."

The cautious, wounded, messed-up-by-Chrissa side of him said that was a good idea. The lonely, emotionally weary version of himself from today didn't want them to leave.

"It's okay. Stay, please. I could use the distraction."

Shock registered on Ivy's pretty features. He must have surprised her as much as he had himself.

Sympathy and softness surfaced next. "Rough day?"

"Something like that."

"Any chance you're interested in some chicken scampi with angel-hair pasta?"

"If that's whatever smells so good, then my answer is yes." Mom had always been the queen of comfort food. Finn felt like he'd been given a strange gift to walk into that happening in his house after the heaviness that had descended on him at the Blairs'.

While Ivy turned chicken in a frying pan, he rested his forearms across the countertop and let his neck fall forward, stretching the tight muscles. Her hand came to rest between his shoulder blades, comforting and confusing.

"You don't have to tell me what happened, but I'm here if you want to."

Tilting his head slightly brought their gazes into alignment. Finn was tired of keeping everything to himself. He'd never been like that before the Chrissa fiasco. Charlie was right—he'd been open to everything before—life and love and community. Now he struggled to share about something as simple as his being upset over the Blairs' situation.

"There's a boy at church—Ryan Blair—who has a rare disease. His dad is in my early-morning men's Bible study, and a handful of us went over to help with some things around the house and to hang shelves in the garage. Ryan's always in pain, but he had a treatment this week that leveled him." He swallowed and blinked to combat his flooding emotions. "A kid should never have to suffer like that."

"Never ever." Moisture shimmered in Ivy's navy eyes. "I saw Ryan listed with his condition on the prayer list in the bulletin at church and felt like I'd been trampled. That's so hard. I'm sorry, Finn."

"Me, too." He inhaled like a shaky leaf clinging to a branch in November. Ivy left her hand between his shoulder blades, her fingers sprawled. She bowed her head, her lids falling shut. Her lips moved as if she was praying, but she didn't speak out loud.

Slowly, the weight lifted and eased.

When she was done, her hand fell away, and for the first time, Finn let himself really see her. "Thank you."

Her smile was tinged with sorrow that matched his. "Anytime."

"How can I help with dinner?"

"There's some bread in the oven. If you can take that out and slice it, that would be great."

Finn did as directed, scavenging for a cutting board that he'd used only a handful of times. "Tell me about your day."

Ivy must have recognized his need for distraction, because she didn't argue. "I'm working on hiring staff for the café right now." She removed the chicken from the pan, plated and covered it. "Charlie asked me to interview Kaia Delaney but said she doesn't want to be directly involved in the decision to hire her because of her relationship with Ryker. So—" her exhale spoke volumes "—I interviewed her today along with a few other candidates. No pressure or anything."

"That's a ton of pressure." Finn understood where Charlie was coming from, but that *was* a lot to put on Ivy.

"We're going to discuss all of the candidates tomorrow, so it's not like the decision is solely mine, but I'm sure my opinion will sway things in a certain direction."

The scent of the bread wafted, igniting Finn's taste buds as he sliced. "At least you're meeting to talk through the options, but yeah, that's a tough one."

Ivy added oil and strips of onions and bell peppers to the pan. "The problem is… I liked Kaia. A lot. She was open about what she's been through—her addiction, losing Honor, battling to gain back custody and to stay clean. I see so much of myself in her. She's a fighter, and I like to think I'm one, too."

"You definitely are."

She paused from stirring the vegetables. "Thank you. Now tell me about the rest of your day. Before the rough ending."

"It was good, actually. C. C. Leap came by today and helped me analyze the land. He was at the cattlemen's dinner. I'm not sure if you remember him. Gray hair. Really bushy eyebrows. Looks like a grouch but he's nice when you talk to him."

"I do remember him." She turned the heat off under the vegetables, leaving them to sit as she poured the sauce she'd made over the pasta that had already finished cooking.

"I'd wondered if the Burkes had overused the land, and according to C.C., this ranch has been used hard for decades. He helped me come up with a plan for dividing grazing into smaller pastures so that grass can regrow. He also suggested I remove the juniper trees. Says they're eating up the water supply."

Ivy stirred the pasta and sauce together, then added the peppers and onions to the mix before adding chicken on top. Finn's taste buds watered as she drizzled the remaining sauce over the chicken and added fresh parmesan cheese.

"That's amazing. You're going to make this ranch so successful, Finn. Of that I have no doubt. Too bad I won't be around to see it."

For all of his frustrations over Ivy and the girls' arrival and extended stay, the reminder that they were leaving after the café opened should be a relief.

The fact that it wasn't made him more than a little concerned.

Chapter Eight

Ivy had the girls pause their movie and wash their hands as she and Finn carried over the dinner items.

Once they were all seated, Finn prayed and then they dug in.

Reese and Lola didn't appreciate the peppers and onions in the dish, covertly shoving them to the side of their plates. Sage wasn't as picky when it came to food.

"I jumped off a wall today." Sage chose a moment with her mouth full of food to announce her feat. "Then I tried to get Lola and Reese to do it, but they were too scaaared." She extended the word, taunting her sisters.

"What kind of wall? And where?"

"At Ms. Lina's. In her backyard."

Ivy was always amazed by the stories the girls told her about their day. Ms. Lina said it was the same at her place—and that some of the things they said about Ivy were hilarious. They'd both agreed not to believe anything outrageous about the other until they'd gone to the source.

"It was only this big, Mommy." Sage had thankfully finished chewing. She held up her hand about three feet off the ground, and Ivy's heart rate went from racing to idling.

"I wasn't scared!" Lola stabbed a piece of chicken with her fork. "I had on my purple flats and I didn't want to get them dirty."

"And I didn't have my sweatshirt on, and I was cold, and besides-ed, Ms. Lina had told us not to, so I went back inside." Reese sniffled at the offense.

"You were both being chickens!" Sage held her fork in the air like a sword, and a wad of pasta flew off it and slid down the table, landing in a heap in front of Finn's plate. Stoically, he scooped them up with his fork and inserted them in his mouth.

The girls erupted in giggles

Lola banged her palm on the table. "Do it again, Mista Finn!"

"Really?" Ivy raised eyebrows at him, torn between humor and exasperation. "You're not helping anything, *Mista Finn.*"

His eyes were full of boyish mischief.

"I do it, too!" Reese had her fork poised and was about to pull back and let the contents fly.

"No." Ivy lunged, stopping her wrist before she could flick the food. "No more." She focused her amused frustration on Finn. "I was *just* about to say that now they're going to think it's funny and all try to do it."

Sage was scooping up another mound of pasta, of course not listening to Ivy in the least.

"Wait." Finn held up a hand. "No more food shenanigans. Listen to your mom, or we'll all get in trouble."

The man was trouble all right.

"What's a shen-i-gan?" Reese asked.

"It's when three little girls mess around." Finn's

pieced-together definition made Ivy smile. There were definitely plenty of shenanigans happening on a daily basis in her life.

"Let's go back to eating the proper way, please. Napkins in our laps. Forks used to put food in our mouths and not anywhere else."

Lola rolled her eyes. "But that's so *boring*, Mommy."

"I know. That's what's so wonderful about it. It's later than we normally eat dinner, so I don't want to hear requests for snacks when we get home. This is it for tonight, so make it count."

"Yes, ma'am." Finn's response earned more giggles from the girls, but then they focused their attention on their food.

Even with Ivy's warning to be sure and eat enough, the girls finished quickly. Their attention spans never lasted long at any meal. She would imagine the first request for a snack would clock in less than thirty minutes from now.

Ivy had them take their plates to the sink and wash their hands.

"Can we watch the rest of our movie? Please?" All three of them asked at once, and Ivy pretended to contemplate her answer even though she'd already planned to say yes.

"Will you be good when it's time for bed? No complaining or crying or staying up late bugging each other?"

Three heads bobbed, sealing the deal.

"Okay, you can finish the movie."

When Ivy turned back to her plate, Finn's cheeks were creased with amusement. "You just got all of that out of them when you were planning to let them watch the movie anyway."

"What makes you say that?"

"You still have laundry going, don't you?"

She gave a sheepish shrug. "I use whatever bargaining tools I can. It's three against one!"

Letting them zone out with a movie tonight had been a mini vacation. A break from the normal routine. They'd all needed the evening off—even Finn, it seemed.

The jolt of panic Ivy had first felt when Finn walked through the door tonight had quickly faded. He'd made things comfortable. If he was faking being okay with them hijacking his house, he was good at it.

And in the process, she'd gotten to do something for him. Something to prove she wasn't here to take, take, take.

"This should be our deal," Ivy said as Finn swiped up sauce with a piece of bread. He'd taken seconds and then thirds. A win in her book. "You won't let me pay anything for using the bunkhouse, so—"

"The place isn't worthy of rent. It's unfinished. Surely you can't argue with that."

"It does make it hard to fight. That's why I'm thinking I'll make another meal for you next week. You like food."

"Caveman like food."

She laughed at his low, gravely delivery. "I really love to cook, so it's not an imposition for me."

"My mom enjoys cooking, too. Charlie? Not so much."

"She has other things occupying her brain. Like running her empires." This time she earned a chuckle from Finn. "Unless you're sick of us, I'm cooking again next week. So you're going to have to be brutally honest with me if you'd rather not have us here."

Finn contemplated, and Ivy found herself holding her breath. "It's not that. Having the girls here…and you here, is great. But the last thing you need is another something on your to-do list. You're raising three three-year-olds, which is enough work on its own. Stop with the payment stuff. Charlie was right—it wasn't like I was using the bunkhouse anyway or renting it out. Besides, it's only for a few more weeks. Just…don't worry about it."

A few more weeks. Things were going fast, that was for sure. When Ivy had said yes to Charlie, six weeks had sounded like a good chunk of time. Now? It was flying by. She was going to miss this place when they moved.

"Let's plan on next Wednesday for dinner."

Finn's eyes crinkled. "I'm not going to win this argument, am I?"

"Not a chance."

"Okay, dinner next Wednesday it is. But just so you know, you've ruined me for my typical fare—which is freezer meals. This was actually quite cruel of you."

"My apologies."

"I'll work on forgiving you." Finn stacked both of their plates and stood. "You cooked. I'll do dishes."

Ivy sat back in surprise. With Lee, she'd always been on her own. Even in marriage, she'd felt disconnected. But after spending time with Finn, she could tell his relationships would operate as a team. A surge of jealousy and yearning surfaced. Someday maybe she'd find that. Someday when her world calmed down and the girls were older. Maybe then she'd take her time and find the right kind of guy. One who also wanted to sign up for raising triplets. She almost snorted out loud. Highly unlikely.

"We'll do the dishes together. It's faster that way."

Finn didn't fight her, so that was what they did. They talked easily, finding a rhythm. Ivy was also going to miss this man when they moved on. He was definitely an anomaly. *Or maybe it's all for show. I can't really know who he is this fast. He could be hiding plenty from me, just like Lee.*

In the beginning, Lee hadn't so much hidden things from her as he'd only shown her one side. Like a girl knowing which angle to pose in for a selfie in order to make herself look good.

And Ivy had been all too willing not to move the camera.

Since she'd made a double batch of the chicken scampi and pasta, Ivy split the leftovers into two and left one in Finn's fridge for him to find the next day.

When she came out from grabbing the last load of laundry, Finn was on the couch and her three girls were literally draped across him. Sage was on the back of the couch tucked against his neck, her fingers a pacifier, Reese was nestled in the crook of his arm, and Lola had taken the liberty of crawling directly into his lap.

"This is what you get for sitting down with them while they're watching a movie." Ivy chose the cushion at the other end of the couch and placed the laundry bin on the coffee table. Maybe she should fold it at home, and they should get out of Finn's way. They'd imposed plenty already, and he'd been incredibly gracious.

"Let's watch the last bit of your movie at home. Okay,

loves?" She tickled the bottom of Reese's foot, earning a giggle and a kick.

"They can finish it here." Finn's response was followed by a yawn. Ivy wasn't sure whether to believe him, but he didn't exactly look uncomfortable.

"Yeah, Mommy." Lola shot her some side-eye from Finn's lap. "Mista Finn says we can finish it here."

"I like Mista Finn's house better than ours." Sage piped up from the back of the couch.

"Me, too," Reese agreed. "And if we leave, Mista Finn would miss the ending."

His smile swung in Ivy's direction, and hers grew to match. "I wouldn't survive not knowing how the movie ends."

"Of course you wouldn't."

Four against one. With the triplets using Finn like a beanbag chair, how was Ivy supposed to argue?

During the remainder of the movie, she didn't see the animation on the screen. She only saw that her girls were falling for Finn. And she was starting to fear that the strange squeeze in her stomach when she was near him or thought about him meant she was treading dangerously close to the same.

In high school, Finn had dated a girl for about six months. Once, when they'd been watching a movie, she'd fallen asleep tucked against his arm. His arm had also fallen asleep. It had been a painfully good place to be, and he hadn't moved even though he'd suffered through the end of that movie.

This time it was three little monkeys who'd taken over his personal space, and once again he was incredibly uncomfortable and strangely content at the same time.

Reese, the most cautious of the three, had snuggled against his side. She'd fallen asleep first, and her little features were so peaceful that his grinch's heart had grown three sizes.

Lola had been trying to make it to the end of the movie, fighting back heavy eyelids and extended yawns, but eventually she'd conked out.

Sage was the only one still standing, though her fidgeting from the back of the couch had lessened considerably.

Ivy returned from the bunkhouse. She'd taken a couple of trips over with laundry as the movie finished and now returned the basket to his laundry room. She walked into the living room as the movie credits rolled and turned off the TV.

"Guess I let them stay up too late." She moved to sit on the coffee table, facing him. "I'll carry Lola and Reese back. Sage, you can walk, can't you, love?"

Sage's weighted lids said the battle to stay awake had been hard-fought. "I hold you, too, Mommy."

Cute. Finn wouldn't mind following that rabbit trail. Wouldn't mind making the same request of Ivy. Despite his determination not to let her burrow under his skin, tonight she'd done exactly that. He'd found himself attending the school of Ivy when she was otherwise distracted. Did she know that she made the tiniest sound popping her lips when she was lost in thought? Or that she tilted her head to the right and only the right when she was listening—and studied the speaker with so much interest that it made them feel like the most important human on the planet?

Stay on track, Brightwood. This isn't your circus. Finn had already bought a ticket to a circus back in

North Dakota, and things hadn't ended well. No need to attend that show again. Especially when the price of admission had cost him so much.

"I'll help carry. I can take two if you take one."

"Thank you. That would be really great. I'd prefer to move them into their beds and keep them asleep if at all possible. If Reese gets woken up she'll start crying and I'm not sure I have the bandwidth for that tonight. Thankfully it's not snowing or freezing, so we don't have to worry about finagling them into jackets."

Ivy gathered the girls' movie and sweatshirts, then slipped Sage from the back of the couch.

Finn scooped up Reese and caught Lola with his other arm. He stood and held still, waiting for complaints. Lola fidgeted and then settled back to peaceful. Reese was so far gone that she didn't even flinch.

These girls. His dry, brittle heart cracked and healed all at the same time. They were good for the soul.

They made their way over to the bunkhouse, a warm spring breeze rustling the night. The sky was filled with so many stars that Finn stumbled trying to take them in. He paused to resituate the girls, whose warm little faces were nestled against his neck.

Thankfully, no one complained or woke.

Not for the first time he wondered how Ivy handled everything with the girls on her own. She was right that it was three against one. And yet, the girls had adjusted quickly to their unexpected time in Westbend—at least from Finn's vantage point.

The woman was definitely doing something right. A lot of things right.

When they reached the bunkhouse, he followed Ivy

YOU pick your books –
WE pay for everything.
You get up to FOUR New Books and TWO Mystery Gifts...absolutely FREE

Dear Reader,

I am writing to announce the launch of a huge **FREE BOOKS GIVEAWAY**... and to let you know that YOU are entitled to choose up to FOUR fantastic books that WE pay for.

Try **Love Inspired® Romance Larger-Print** books and fall in love with inspirational romances that take you on an uplifting journey of faith, forgiveness and hope.

Try **Love Inspired® Suspense Larger-Print** books where courage and optimism unite in stories of faith and love in the face of danger.

Or TRY BOTH!

In return, we ask just one favor: Would you please participate in our brief Reader Survey? We'd love to hear from you.

This FREE BOOKS GIVEAWAY means that we pay for *everything!* We'll even cover the shipping, and no purchase is necessary, now or later. So please return your survey today. You'll get **Two Free Books** and **Two Mystery Gifts** from each series to try, altogether worth over **$20!**

Sincerely

Pam Powers

Pam Powers
For Harlequin Reader Service

Complete the survey below and return it today to receive up to 4 FREE BOOKS and FREE GIFTS guaranteed!

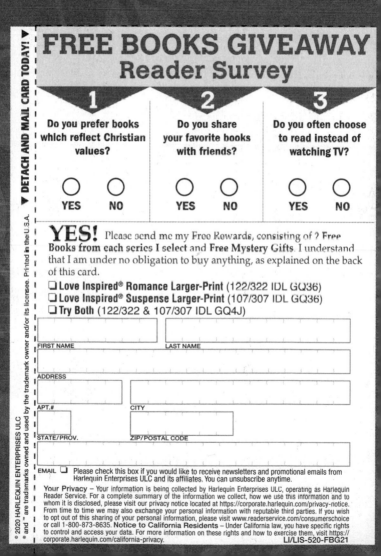

▼ DETACH AND MAIL CARD TODAY! ▼

FREE BOOKS GIVEAWAY
Reader Survey

1

Do you prefer books which reflect Christian values?

◯ YES   ◯ NO

2

Do you share your favorite books with friends?

◯ YES   ◯ NO

3

Do you often choose to read instead of watching TV?

◯ YES   ◯ NO

YES! Please send me my Free Rewards, consisting of 2 Free Books from each series I select and **Free Mystery Gifts**. I understand that I am under no obligation to buy anything, as explained on the back of this card.

❑ Love Inspired® Romance Larger-Print (122/322 IDL GQ36)
❑ Love Inspired® Suspense Larger-Print (107/307 IDL GQ36)
❑ Try Both (122/322 & 107/307 IDL GQ4J)

FIRST NAME   LAST NAME

ADDRESS

APT.#   CITY

STATE/PROV.   ZIP/POSTAL CODE

EMAIL ❑ Please check this box if you would like to receive newsletters and promotional emails from Harlequin Enterprises ULC and its affiliates. You can unsubscribe anytime.

LI/LIS-520-FBG21

▲ If offer card is missing write to: Harlequin Reader Service, P.O. Box 1341, Buffalo, NY 14240-8531 or visit www.ReaderService.com ▲

BUSINESS REPLY MAIL
FIRST-CLASS MAIL   PERMIT NO. 717   BUFFALO, NY

POSTAGE WILL BE PAID BY ADDRESSEE

HARLEQUIN READER SERVICE
PO BOX 1341
BUFFALO NY 14240-8571

NO POSTAGE
NECESSARY
IF MAILED
IN THE
UNITED STATES

into the bunkroom. She placed Sage on the top bunk, then motioned to the bottom.

"They can both go here. That way if they don't realize where they are and fall out, it's not a huge deal."

Spoken like a veteran mom. Finn knelt, and Ivy helped him finagle both girls into the bunk. They snuggled under the blanket she covered them with, Lola's nose wrinkling, Reese's mug snarling at the disruption to her sleep.

He and Ivy retreated to the living room space of the bunkhouse, and she shut the girls' door behind them.

"I feel like I should get some sort of newbie award since neither of my passengers woke up on my first transfer attempt." As if there would be more transfer attempts? This was why he hadn't wanted Ivy and the girls to stay at the ranch. He got involved too easily.

And now they'd made plans for another dinner next week. Yes, he wanted whatever food Ivy created. He even wanted the companionship. But he shouldn't. He knew too well this road terminated in a dead end.

Ivy was handling her life on her own, and Finn needed to let her continue that…without his involvement.

"You certainly have your hands full, Ivy Darling."

Her smile was worn but content. "I wouldn't have it any other way. When we learned we were having triplets, at first I didn't believe the doctor. I made him repeat it three times, ironically. It took me about a day to get over the shock, and then I was just excited. I knew they were meant to be. Can you even imagine not having one of them? Life wouldn't be the same."

"They're definitely all perfectly unique."

"Exactly. You get them better than Lee did, and

you've only known them a short time." She slapped a hand over her mouth, her eyes wide.

The compliment came with a wallop of pain. How could their father not have seen the girls for the gifts they were?

"I'm sorry," Ivy continued. "I try very hard not to speak badly of Lee, mostly for my own sanity. I can't live with negativity permeating my world, even if he did make terrible decisions."

Finn should take lessons from her. The stuff with Chrissa was so much less than what she'd suffered through because of her husband, and yet, she could be a motivational speaker.

"How did you get there? And so fast?" She'd told him Lee had taken his life a little over a year ago.

"Lots of counseling and letting myself feel all the things. Plus, the girls. Even if I hadn't wanted to process everything in a healthy way for myself, I did it for them. But along the way, I started doing it for me."

"Maybe instead of making another meal next week, you should be coaching me on how to move on." He'd said too much. And yet, Ivy had a certain vulnerability and humbleness that said she could be trusted.

"What do you need to heal from, Finn Brightwood?" The question was soft, her head doing that endearing tilt, her eyes asking him to spill. "Was that why you were against us staying here when Charlie came up with the idea? Because you're not that person as far as I can tell. Sometimes you try to act tough or aloof, but at the core...I think you're one of the best people I've ever met."

I think. A trace of doubt joined that phrase, as if Ivy was almost certain, but he was playing the part just enough to confuse her. Probably better that way. Finn had been too easily swayed in the past. Too eager to help. Too willing to ignore the red flags.

"There was a woman." If he told her some of it, he could build the wall between them again that had started crumbling tonight. "Back in North Dakota when I was working an oil rig. The way things ended really messed with my head." More detail didn't jump from his tongue. How could he tell Ivy the truth behind him trying to rescue Chrissa and failing when that was exactly why he was avoiding growing feelings for her? "She and the situation broke something in me, and I'm not sure how to patch it."

It was the truth, just not all of it. But since the whole truth would wound, he kept it tucked close.

Ivy squeezed his arm. "I'm sorry. Thank you for telling me." And then instead of letting go, she stepped closer. Her arms slid around his middle and her cheek pressed against his chest. "Thank you for your help with the girls tonight. And for letting us crash your evening. It was over and above."

His arms, which had automatically wrapped around her in response, squeezed. "You're welcome. Thank you for dinner." He was glad he could help her out—as long as he didn't emotionally lose himself in the process like he had the last time.

As Ivy eased back from their impromptu embrace, their eyes met and held. A current passed between them that surprised him but also felt as natural as taking his next breath.

He'd been attracted to her from the start, but keeping his distance had allowed him to ignore that niggling sensation.

Tonight had obliterated that space.

He rested his wrists on her shoulders, unwilling to break their connection so fast. His hands itched to slide under her hair, and his mouth…it had other objectives.

He wanted to kiss her, and the shock of that revelation nearly leveled him.

"I—" He swallowed, certain his expression was detailing his every thought and desire.

The skin meeting her pretty eyes crinkled, and her hands came up, hooking over his arms, resting there, holding him in place.

"Me, too."

So she did know. And she felt the same interest. Resisting the implications of that knowledge was like attempting to swim in a frigid mountain stream instead of pulling himself out onto the warm, sun-kissed bank.

They stayed frozen in time, each warring internally.

Finally, Finn's resolve snapped into place. "I can't do this." He removed his arms, causing her hands to plummet.

He couldn't sway from his original plan. It would never work.

"I—"

"You're leaving." He cut her off because he was afraid that if she disagreed with him, if she expressed interest at all, he wouldn't have the strength to say no. He wouldn't be able to resist her. And he really couldn't go *there* again with someone whose life was in disarray. "I've been messed with before. I can't do that again."

"Finn." His name snapped from her tongue as if she was reprimanding one of the girls.

He took a step back, then another, bumping into a chair.

"Finn!"

He ignored her call, not waiting for the rest of what she had to say. Instead, like a coward, he turned tail and ran.

Chapter Nine

The next afternoon, Finn drove into town at his sister's request. Supposedly she needed help with some things at the café, though he wasn't sure why his presence was necessary.

She was capable of most everything herself.

And she also had Ryker. Or Ivy. Or even Scott, who was a mechanic in her shop.

Something smelled fishy.

At least she'd asked for his help *before* the situation had developed with Ivy last night, so he knew it wasn't about that. Though he could use a stern reprimand. What had he been thinking getting so close to her? Almost kissing her? Ivy and the girls staying at the ranch complicated things and forced them into the same proximity. She was a good person working on changing her life. Finn just couldn't be involved in that process again.

Last night as he'd tossed and turned, he'd tried to wrap his mind around how things between them had escalated so quickly. He'd concluded that it had something to do with the scene he'd walked in on when he'd returned from the Blairs'.

Being around Ivy and the girls had made him want more of the same. A family to come home to. A wife to pray with him. Kids to raise and love. He'd been fighting feeling anything for anyone since Chrissa, but in that process, he'd denied his desire to have a family one day.

He wanted more nights like last night, but they couldn't be with Ivy and her girls. They were moving to California, and Finn wouldn't be the one to stop them. Between her parents, her late husband and the girls, she had plenty to work through, and Finn had meant it when he'd decided no more rescuing, no more messy relationships. But he'd forgotten that he did want something good and easy. That had to exist, right?

He arrived at the café. Inside, he found his sister and no Ivy. It was just after four. Perhaps she'd already gone home. Relief made his limbs buzz.

There was a chance he'd told Charlie he couldn't come into town until this time so that he wouldn't run into Ivy.

There was also a chance he was turning into a wuss.

Charlie greeted him, "Hey, brother." She squinted in his direction. "What was the massive sigh for?"

Oops. He hadn't meant to broadcast his blatant relief. "Nothing. What's going on with you? What do you need help with?"

She paused as if considering continuing her line of questioning, but after two beats of analyzing, she pointed to a stack of pictures that were propped against the wall.

"I need to hang those, and I could use a hand."

That made absolutely no sense. "You need me to help you hang pictures?"

She nodded fast like hummingbird wings.

"Don't you have a boyfriend for this kind of stuff? Hanging pictures definitely seems like it would fall into the *special friend* category."

Charlie laughed at the title their parents had given to anyone either of them had dated…not that Charlie had done a lot of that before Ryker.

"He's at work."

"What about Ivy?"

"She has other things to do."

"Scott could help you."

"Scott's busy being a mechanic, which is his job."

"And yours. Plus, I've never known you not to be capable on your own. You don't need me for this. What's going on?"

Charlie crossed her arms. "I miss you, okay? Everything's been so busy we never see each other."

His radar said that wasn't the full truth, but Finn played along. "And whose fault is that?"

"Mine. I can't help it if I'm successful."

Finn groaned and rolled his eyes, and Charlie's delighted laughter punctuated his annoyance. Something was still definitely fishy, but his sister would spill soon enough. She was nothing if not blunt, and she was terrible at hiding her feelings.

He picked up the first piece of art. It was a black-and-white photo of a table with a steaming coffee mug perched on it. "All right. Let's get this done. Where do we start?"

"Over here." She motioned to the corner, and he followed. "We need to measure and map this out. There are ten photos, and of course I need them balanced."

"Of course."

Charlie did some quick math on a piece of paper. "Hold the picture up, would you? I'm trying to decide how high I want them." He obeyed. "Up a little." He inched it toward the ceiling. "Nope. That's too far. Down." At this point, the triplets could be handling Charlie's request. "There! That's it." He hadn't even moved the picture again.

Charlie measured up from the floor and jotted down the height she wanted. "Can you grab the hammer and nails? They're on the counter."

Finn did as she'd asked, handing them over. "What is going on, Char? I know you didn't ask me into town for this."

"Which one should go next? The landscape or Main Street? Did I tell you a local artist took these? She's letting me display them, and I'm going to keep her information on the bulletin board in case anyone wants to purchase one. Win-win."

"It doesn't matter. Once we have the nails in place, you can switch them around. As you well know."

"Fine." The hammer swung down by her hip as she turned to face him. "You're not going to like what I have to say."

Finn's pulse revved into high gear. Had something happened with Ivy? Had she quit because of last night? What if she'd told Charlie and his sister blamed him? No. That couldn't be. Charlie had asked him to help before anything had almost happened between him and Ivy.

"I need a favor from you."

"This is a favor."

Charlie's head shook, her eyes worried. "A bigger favor."

Oh, boy.

"I've decided to use the opening night of the café to raise funds for a charity that provides physical items for foster kids."

"That's great."

"And I'm going to hold an auction as part of it."

"What kind of auction?" As a rancher, there wasn't much he could donate. Was there?

"The kind that lets women bid on hanging out with a guy."

A slow churn began in his gut. "You mean a bachelor auction? The kind where women ogle men and then bid on a date with them?"

She winced. "Sort of. We're also pitching it for women who'd like to have a handyman help them out with some things, so it's not all romantic. There will be women interested in both options."

And she wanted him to be involved. That was why she'd asked him here. She'd known that if she texted or called him, he'd say no. Well, she was about to hear the same in person.

"No way. I'm not doing it, and you're crazy for even attempting it. You're never going to get enough guys to do it."

"I already have eleven lined up. Most of them took very little convincing. But eighteen women have signed up for a bidding number so far, so I really need to round up more men to even things out."

"How long have you been planning this?"

"A week."

She worked fast. He'd give her that. "And when were you planning to ask me to be part of it?"

"Never, actually. I'd hoped I wouldn't need you because I thought you'd make a big stink about it."

"You were right."

"It's a few hours of your life, Finn, and it's for a great cause. I can send you information about the charity. It's really amazing. You know it's been hard for me to step back from fostering because of how busy things are with the shop and the café. This is something I can do in the meantime to love on some kids."

What irony. Yes, he'd just considered finding someone to share his life with, but this definitely wasn't what he'd had in mind for how to go about it.

"At least say you'll consider it. Don't say no right away."

"That's your favorite negotiating tactic, isn't it?"

Charlie's grin was far too knowing and far too victorious. Her phone beeped in her pocket, and she checked it.

"Scott has an issue with a customer next door." She motioned to the photos. "Finish hanging those, would you? I've got to run over there."

Finn shook his head at her retreating figure. This was why he was so afraid of getting pulled into another mismatched, drama-filled relationship. Because he was a pushover.

A few minutes later, Finn heard the back door of the café open and then footsteps echoing down the hallway. He was in the middle of pounding in a nail, so he didn't turn.

"Anything else, Your Highness? You know, with all of your businesses, you should really be able to hire people to do this stuff." Though of course Charlie had pulled him in because of the auction request. And now kept him working because she could.

"I really prefer *Your Majesty*." Ivy paused next to the counter. She was dressed in a red sweater, dark jeans and ankle boots. At the sight of her, his mouth filled with dry sand. "And since none of the aforementioned businesses are mine, I can't hire anyone to do the little things."

His arms fell to his sides, the hammer heavy in his hand. "Hey."

"Hi." They stared at each other for a few beats, two teenagers at a loss for how to communicate, and then Ivy rounded the counter and opened the laptop stationed on the cabinets that lined the back wall.

Not knowing what to say or do, Finn returned to measuring and pounding nails, their almost kiss as fresh in his mind as laundry hung outside to dry. He added pictures so he could check how it looked, stepping back to survey his work.

"The one second from the right is crooked."

He squinted, trying to find the infraction.

Ivy strode past him and made an adjustment. On her trek back to her safe haven behind the counter, Finn snaked out a hand and captured her wrist, gently pulling her to a stop.

"What's going on? You okay?"

"I'm fine, Finn." Her tone, which sizzled and hissed, said otherwise.

"I thought… I know we almost…" He couldn't bring himself to say *kissed* out loud. "But I thought we were good. That we decided not to go down that road."

She gave a very un-Ivy-like snort.

Finn was obviously missing something, but he had

no idea what. He liked having Charlie for a sister—at least when she wasn't asking him for favors he had no interest in fulfilling—because she broadcasted everything for all the world to see.

Ivy was a vault. If she hadn't just snipped at him, her smooth features would have hidden her upset.

Finn wasn't sure what to do with the woman whose wrist he couldn't seem to remove his hand from. Ask what was wrong? Or turn tail and run...again?

We? There'd been no *we* in last night's discussion. Finn somehow remembered them coming to a joint decision, but all Ivy recalled was his quick retreat and the numerous times he'd cut her off. He hadn't let her get a word in edgewise, and then he'd bolted from the bunkhouse.

Who was Finn Brightwood to tell her how to feel and when to feel it? Ivy had cowered plenty during her marriage, disagreeing with Lee but going along because she hadn't wanted to rock the boat.

Well, she wasn't that same person anymore. The younger version of herself had possessed a backbone. The current version of herself was more than ready to take that skeleton out of the closet, dust it off and bring it back to life.

"Mommy!" Sage, Reese and Lola broke through the back door of the café, and Ivy's muscles switched from hard and angry to pliable and tender in an instant. She knelt to catch the girls' hugs.

Ms. Lina followed behind them, and after squeezing the triplets, Ivy stood to greet her.

"Thank you for dropping them off."

"Of course. I knew I had to run some errands tonight—

I need to grab a few things at the five-and-dime and then hit Len's Grocery—so I figured dropping off the girls would force me to make that happen since shopping isn't my favorite. Your car was unlocked, so I left their car seats in the back."

"Perfect, thanks." Ivy had been outside unlocking her car when Finn must have arrived. She'd found so much trash and smashed snacks in the back seat that she'd spent a few minutes cleaning it out. Charlie had told Ivy she'd asked her brother to stop by the café today. But once it neared four and he still hadn't shown, Ivy had begun wondering if Finn was trying to avoid her.

But that was a crazy idea. Especially since Finn thought they were "fine" or "good" or whatever he'd labeled them.

Lina left, and Ivy gave the girls another squeeze. She was enjoying her work at the café so much, but seeing her girls was still the best part of her day.

"All right, loves, we can head home soon. I just have to send an email before we go. Do you think you can entertain yourselves for a couple of minutes?"

She scanned the space. What would they do with themselves? There was nowhere for them to be. Nothing for them to do. The tables were adult-sized. They should really have a kids' corner. Especially if Charlie wanted to use the café as a place for her mechanic shop patrons to wait and work. Ivy made a mental note to talk to Charlie about the idea.

"The girls can help me hang pictures." Finn's blueberry eyes met hers, full of questions. "If that would help."

Ivy wanted to refuse Finn's offer, especially after last night and her remaining upset, but she pressed her teeth tight to avoid a negative answer. "Sure, that would be great. Thank you." Her wooden tone contradicted the words.

The faster she sent the email, the faster she could remove herself from Finn's presence. Ivy was in the middle of finalizing the menu with a local bakery they'd contracted to make muffins, scones and cookies. They planned to rotate through something new each week until they found the most popular items, which they'd then carry consistently.

Ivy and Charlie both liked that they were supporting another local business.

"Mommy said you holded us home cause we were all sleepy." Lola's tone was part pouting, part curiosity.

"That's right," Finn answered. "But you sure tried your best to stay awake, didn't you?"

"I did!"

"*I* didn't fall asleep," Sage retorted. "I was a big girl." Outside of yesterday, when she'd succumbed to a nap and Lola hadn't, Sage was usually the one who managed to stay awake the longest.

"Nothing wrong with sleep." Finn's gentle response held humor, and a piece of Ivy's anger that had formed last night chipped away like a chunk of glacier crashing into the ocean.

He asked about the girls' day, and Ivy listened with one ear as they chimed in with answers. Her fingers danced across the keys, writing a sentence and then deleting it. She was having a hard time concentrating, with the chatter going on behind her.

Reese told Finn that Ms. Lina had let the girls take her bunny outside today since the weather had been warm, and Finn's questions and attention to the shyest of her three girls melted another wedge of ice.

Ever since the girls had helped Finn with the chicks, they checked on them every day. If they were allowed or had the space, they'd no doubt want a whole farm full of animals. But that wouldn't happen in her parents' pristine home. Ivy's mom did have a dog, but he was older and not a fan of children, so she doubted he'd be much of a playmate for the girls.

Today Ivy's phone had buzzed numerous times with texts from her mom.

Managed to get the girls a spot for summer tennis! The rest of the message had gone on to explain how her mother had a connection at the club who'd pulled a few strings for her. Ivy had typed back I DON'T WANT THE GIRLS IN TENNIS, in all caps, and then left it unsent while her frustration skyrocketed.

Mom had also notified Ivy of some updates regarding the pretentious preschool she'd chosen for the girls—not that Ivy got a say in the matter—and that she was remodeling what would be the girls' bedroom into something *calm* and *soothing*.

Hopefully those weren't code words for how she expected the triplets to behave.

If only Ivy could give the girls the freedom of living at the ranch or somewhere like it, running wild and experiencing the wide-open spaces full-time. The more she watched them blossom in Westbend, the more she wanted that kind of independence for them in the future.

Lola appeared at her side and tugged on her arm. "Mommy, we waited *forever*, but we're all done now."

Done with Finn already? Maybe he wasn't the exciting toy he'd shown the promise of being back when the girls had first discovered him. Ivy's mouth itched to curve, but she stemmed the response just as Charlie came through the back door of the café.

"My favorite triplets!" She high-fived each of them as they ran to greet her. "What's new, girls?"

"We have to wait for Mommy to work," Sage huffed with impatience.

Reese sniffled as if the situation warranted tears.

Lola spun in a circle, making her skirt flare. "Do you see my skirt, Ms. Charlie?"

"Love the skirt." Charlie's smile bloomed. "And how terrible for the three of you, having to wait!"

They nodded gravely, appreciating that Charlie would take them seriously even though she was tamping down amusement.

"What do you have left?" she asked Ivy. "You can take off and I can finish up."

"I just need to confirm our choices with the bakery." *And instead of sending the email, I've been over here distracted by Finn, the girls, thoughts of my parents...*

"Okay, then why don't I take the girls out back to the sandbox while you do that?"

The girls cheered and jumped up and down.

"Are you sure?" Ivy would fight her boss, but she'd quickly learned that Charlie had a huge heart for kids and truly enjoyed the triplets. It was easy to picture her loving Honor well as her foster mom, and when Charlie and Ryker started a family someday, she'd no doubt be an amazing mother.

"Absolutely. Come on!" Charlie held out her hands and the girls grabbed hold. She spared her brother's work a parting glance. "Finn, the one on the left is crooked."

Ivy chuckled silently as the four of them exited through the back door and the café returned to peace and quiet. Except for Finn's groan, which made her laugh more.

How could he amuse her and make her mad at the same time? And who was he? The snarly guy she'd first met? Or the sweet one from last night who had caused unexpected feelings for him to buoy to the surface? Obviously the same had happened for him, though he'd been unwilling to admit it outside of the implication that he'd wanted to kiss her.

Part of Ivy's attraction to him last night *had* to be because she missed seeing the girls with a father figure in their lives. Didn't it? Okay, she wasn't sure of that, but she was grasping for a reason—any reason—that she'd let herself slide so easily in Finn's direction. In the direction of Finn's lips, to be more exact. Because the pull to kiss him… Ivy fanned herself with her hand. It had been strong.

"Warm?"

She whirled to find Finn standing behind the opposite counter, far too close for comfort.

"Something like that." Amazingly, the words didn't wobble like her pulse.

"You planning to tell me what's going on with you? My best guess is that it has something to do with last night, but then again, it could have nothing to do with me. You could have had a rough day at work. Your boss could be a jerk. Your boss's brother could be a jerk. You could be suffocating from small-town gossip. You could—"

"Okay, okay." Amusement bubbled despite her annoyance with him.

His mouth quirked as if this was all fun and games.

It wasn't for her. An almost kiss meant something. She hadn't planned to get anywhere near a *shenanigan* like that, but yet they'd stumbled right into the thick of it. Which meant she had to deal with the why of it. She'd learned after losing Lee that burying her emotions and reactions didn't work.

It was one thing for her to agree that it was illogical for her and Finn to enter into any kind of romantic relationship. But having Finn dictate to her that they couldn't be an item when she hadn't been able to get a word in edgewise? That had hurt.

"I just… I didn't appreciate that you made the decision for us last night without any input from me. Believe it or not, I'm not interested in having anything develop with you, either, Finn. Not only are we moving to California soon, but I have a lot going on with the girls. My focus is on them and being the best mom possible. I have reservations, too, and I came to that conclusion on my own. You didn't have to make it all about you." Oops. She might have gone a little too far with that last bit, but at the same time, it felt good to speak her truth. She'd failed at that over the years, so learning how to stand up for herself again—without overdoing it—might take some time.

Finn's mouth hung open for a couple seconds before he snapped it shut. And then he ran a hand across the back of his neck. "I'm an idiot. You're right. I didn't listen to what you had to say, and I'm sorry."

Oh. She'd expected more of a fight out of him. She'd geared herself up for one, at least. But Finn never ceased to surprise her.

"Thank you." She was supposed to be writing an email while the girls were outside with Charlie. Instead she was staring at Finn, questioning what it would have felt like if the two of them had let that kiss happen.

"So…should we cancel dinner next week? It's okay if you need some space from me. *I* might need some space from me right now." His head shook. "I feel like a jerk, Ivy. I'm sorry I stuck my boot in my mouth."

His sincerity and the country-boy charm that seeped from his pores as easily as dust blew over the dry Colorado terrain softened her. She liked being around Finn. The girls adored him. What would another meal together hurt? Especially when their time in Westbend was going so quickly. It could be a farewell/thank-you dinner of sorts as the café would be opening in two weeks, and the week after that, Ivy planned to continue on her way to California with the girls.

"Let's still do it."

"I would argue with that, but the thought of whatever you plan to make is compelling me not to." Finn's grin melted the last of her reserves. "You'll have to tell me what to bring or buy for dinner."

"You're providing the house and kitchen. That's plenty."

His eyes narrowed. "Doesn't seem fair."

"It isn't a decision you get to make. I'm in charge of dinner."

"All right." His calloused palms rose in defense. "You win."

"I've been winning a lot lately. I think I'm on a streak."

"You definitely are. Especially since I'm afraid to cross you. Made a mistake yesterday and got reprimanded for it. Rightfully so." Finn's low chuckle delighted her more than it should.

"Someone has to keep you in line."

"Cavemen need direction. What can I say? I'm not trained socially, it seems."

Ivy was enjoying this lighter turn in conversation, glad that she and Finn could stumble their way back to safer, more agreeable ground.

He morphed into serious mode, but his twinkling eyes gave away his mirth. "I'm very much looking forward to whatever it is you make next week, Ivy Darling. And if you need me to pick something up, please let me know."

Ivy barely resisted a curtsy in response to his regal tone. "I mean…if you *insist* on participating, you could see if the bakery has anything chocolate on hand for dessert. The girls would lose their minds over a treat."

"And you?"

"Same."

His hearty laugh warmed her insides and created an inkling of worry. *Was* spending time with Finn a good idea? Or should they go their separate ways?

It's only three weeks.

True. How much could even happen in that short amount of time?

Chapter Ten

Can you at least give me a hint?

The next Wednesday, Ivy pocketed the text from Finn with a laugh and then retrieved a pint-size table from the back of her Suburban, snaking it through the front door of the café.

Ever since she'd told Finn this week's dinner was going to be a surprise, he'd been trying to get her to give up the secret.

She placed the table in the corner where a small book and toy case already perched, and retrieved her phone.

You'll know tonight. And you're making too big of a deal out of this. Who knows if you'll even like it?

Though she would imagine the recipe of his mom's roast would be a hit, Ivy couldn't be certain. If she'd known that a small surprise would bug Finn this much, she would have started tormenting him sooner.

She returned to her vehicle for the small colorful chairs. The bright yellow and turquoise looked great in the space, and she could imagine her girls coloring, reading or playing in the kids' corner. She could also picture moms stopping in for coffee, delighted to have a place their kids could hang out in at the same time.

The mayor of Westbend had popped in this week to see how things were progressing, and Ivy had pitched him her idea of having the café available for evening meetings. Bill Bronson had liked the suggestion, commenting that the city council could take advantage of the option—especially on nights when there would be a large turnout of Westbend citizens attending the meetings.

After getting approval for her idea from Charlie, Ivy had set up a scheduling calendar online for meeting options, and a few dates were already filled.

If Ivy left the café with anything, it would hopefully be a steady stream of customers all primed and ready to use the space that had turned out beautifully.

Charlie's vision was minimalistic—black-and-white with touches of raw brick and warm wood. Farmhouse shabby chic. Ivy had found wire baskets to house the silverware and napkins, and they'd gone with mugs of varying colors for coffee and tea. She'd also found a cooler for drinks that was new but looked vintage. That was humming along at the end of the counter, and Ivy had placed an order for glass bottle options to fill it.

She loved that Charlie's Pit Stop had a vintage vibe. She loved that the sign outside had the same old-fashioned look as Charlie's Garage next door. She loved that the café was really coming together, and the realization that she wouldn't get to stay to see it blossom stung more than she cared to admit.

Her phone buzzed with a text. Finn had sent her a

GIF of a caveman saying *Me like food*. She was still laughing when his next text quickly followed. When are you starting training?

Tomorrow.

After numerous conversations with Charlie, they'd decided George and Kaia were the best hires for the café. Kaia was ecstatic about the opportunity, and so far Ivy had no qualms about hiring her. George was in his sixties and very personable, and with his more flexible schedule, he'd also be a good fit.

Finn sent the prayer emoji back, and Ivy's tight muscles unwound. Such a simple thing to have someone praying for her, and yet, she'd never experienced it in this way.

"Hello!" Charlie hurried in the front door wearing her mechanic coveralls and carrying what looked to be the new point-of-sale system.

"Good! It got here in time." Crazy to think that in one week, they'd have the soft opening. When Ivy had said yes to Charlie, she'd never imagined things would go so fast…or that she'd enjoy it all so much.

"I rushed it." Charlie plunked the box on the counter. "I was too nervous to chance it being late." She turned and saw the kids' space. "Oh, it looks amazing!" She crossed over and ran her hand along the small bookcase that also housed games and toys. "How did you find these vintage toys? They fit the style of the place perfectly."

"Some were at the thrift store in town, and others I found online."

"You're so good at keeping the theme of the café

going in every detail. If I had known that before I hired you, I wouldn't have given you a choice to go or stay. I would have forced you to commit." Charlie dropped into one of the kids' chairs and stretched her legs out in front of her. "Thank you for not only thinking of this corner but orchestrating it." Ivy had priced out the concept before even mentioning it to Charlie. It was an easy thing to do when she trusted that her boss was open to suggestions.

"You're welcome. Thanks for appreciating my ideas."

"Always. Are you ready for tomorrow?"

Tomorrow the four of them were being trained on the espresso machine over an online video conferencing call. And then Charlie planned to teach them the ins and outs of the payment processing system since she used the same kind next door.

"I don't know I want to say yes, but then my stomach does jumping jacks and tells me I'm not ready for anything."

Charlie's cheeks creased. "I'm nervous, too. Honor calls it nervouscited. I'd say that's a fitting description of my current mood."

"Me, too. I keep wondering what we've missed." Even though Ivy had followed the detailed planning from Charlie's original manager, there would be things that slipped through the cracks. If only she knew what those were so she could troubleshoot now.

"When or if something goes wrong, we'll deal with it and figure it out. At least we're having a soft opening. People won't get as upset if something is off, because they know that's the night we're working out kinks."

"And the bachelor auction should distract from any issues."

Charlie laughed. "Right? Ryker thinks I'm crazy for doing it."

Honestly, Ivy had thought the same thing. The event could go either way—it could make a lot of people happy or a lot of people uncomfortable.

"Are you planning to have George or Kaia be in charge until you find a new manager? Or are you going to manage them? How's the hunt going?"

Charlie winced. "Actually…I've been meaning to talk to you about that." Hiring a new café manager was something Charlie had said she would handle, so Ivy had been uninvolved with the process so far. "I had an ad out, but all of the responses I received were completely unqualified."

"I'm completely unqualified. If you hadn't had the business set-up plan from Tammy, I never would have been able to pull any of this off. So maybe you should look into some of them anyway."

"You're not unqualified. You've handled everything with the setup like a pro. I honestly don't know what I would have done without you. My mechanic business would have faltered for sure because I would have been running ragged trying to do everything myself. The thought of you leaving makes me hyperventilate." Charlie bent her knees and wrapped her arms around them. "Ivy…have you ever considered staying in Westbend? Living here? Because if that has ever crossed your radar, I would ask you to run the café in a heartbeat. I've been biting my tongue, trying not to mention the idea because I know your original plan to move to your parents' still stands. But I can't stop myself from at least seeing if you'd consider staying."

Shock had Ivy's body crumpling into the tiny chair

across from Charlie. What in the world? She would never have fathomed Charlie was harboring a notion like that. "I...I don't know what to say."

"I realize it's a long shot, but you've done such an amazing job getting the café ready. I hate to lose you. I'm definitely not going to be offended if you say no to staying, but will you think about it?"

"I will." It only made sense to let the offer sink in and process it overnight. Sleeping on something was always a good idea. Though she didn't see it as a real possibility, did she? Could she manage the girls and make enough to support them without family and help? Staying for six weeks—seven if she included the week she'd waited for her vehicle to be fixed—was one thing, but staying indefinitely was entirely another, presenting far more challenges. Ms. Lina had only agreed to a short-term gig. Although...the girls could start pre-school in the fall. It wouldn't be the prestigious one her mom had in mind, but they had made friends in West-bend and thoroughly enjoyed the kids in their Sunday school class. They'd probably love it.

I'm jumping too far into the future. Now wasn't the time to dissect the bomb Charlie had just detonated. Ivy would do it later. Maybe while making dinner tonight... or perhaps after, when Finn could help her process.

Just when Ivy thought she had it all together, Charlie had come along and thrown *another* wrench in her plans. And the hope that had ignited at her offer... Ivy didn't know what to do about that. At all.

Finn had been banished from his own kitchen.

He'd come in from the ranch to find the girls coloring in the living room and Ivy bustling around the kitchen, and his traitor heart had skipped rope like an elementary kid in a competition.

Immediately Ivy had begun clucking at him. "Out! You can't be in here. Put your blinders on." She'd made a shooing motion in his direction, as if he'd been rushing the gates of the kitchen when he'd only been taking off his coat and boots and storing them.

"Yes, ma'am." He'd cleaned up from working and now returned to the front of the house. "Are you sure I can't do anything to help?"

"No. Now quit being nice and get out of here."

His chest vibrated with quiet laughter at the reprimand. Whatever she was making smelled like home and childhood and comfort food, so he knew well enough to keep quiet and stay out of her way. He definitely didn't want to get punished for disobeying.

Finn went into the living room and dropped to a seat on the couch, letting out a groan at his complaining muscles. Between calving season and working on the list of items C.C. had suggested to get the ranch back to optimum performance, he fell into bed each night and slept hard. When he'd settled on the idea of owning his own ranch, he hadn't realized the kind of mental and physical strength it would take. He felt like one of the calves. Like he was wobbling around on weak legs and a strong gust of wind could take him down.

The girls weren't watching a movie this time. Instead, each had a coloring book, and markers were spread across the coffee table.

"Look at my flower, Mista Finn." Lola held the purple and pink petals up for his inspection.

"It's beautiful. Good job, Lo."

"Look at mine next!" Reese's ability to stay between

the lines wasn't as pronounced as Lola's, but her page was definitely bright and happy.

"Also well done. You girls are little artists."

They beamed, then bent their heads to continue their work.

"Don't look at mine until it's done." Sage laid an arm over her drawing to block his access.

Finn held up a palm. "Promise I won't look."

Sage studied him for a moment as if gauging whether she should trust his response. Then she went back to work, her arm removed from the drawing again.

Finn held in a chuckle. Sage would be offended if she knew he found her and her sisters amusing. His world was sure going to turn quiet and uneventful again once the three of them—four of them—left for California.

"How's your week been?" Ivy asked from her perch between the counter and the island. She was pouring drinks now and moving some kind of bread into a serving dish.

"Good, for the most part. Busy." Finn shared some of what he'd accomplished from C.C.'s suggestions. He did not share, however, that he'd been on a date this week. In the interest of following through on his thoughts after his impromptu dinner with Ivy and the girls last week of wanting to find a partner and have a family someday, Finn had asked out a woman from church. She was smart and successful. Pretty, too. He hadn't known if they would be a good fit, so he'd asked her out for coffee, thinking that way if they weren't a match, they wouldn't be stuck with each other for a whole meal.

They weren't a match.

Finn had never been so grateful to finish a cup of coffee. The conversation had been stilted and hard to come by. The woman had spoken negatively about so many things that Finn had lost count. It had left him missing the chatter of the girls and the easy dialogue and banter he had with Ivy.

Not good.

Not good at all.

He could tell Ivy about the date—it wasn't as if *they* were dating—but something held him back. Probably the fact that he'd implied that Chrissa hurting him was what kept him from relationships when that wasn't the whole truth.

What Chrissa had been going through was a big piece of the puzzle. And if he told Ivy that, he'd wound her, because she would decipher he had the same concerns about her.

"How was your day?"

"Crazy. I'll tell you about it later." Her vision bounced to the girls, communicating that she couldn't talk about whatever had happened in front of them.

Now he was intrigued.

Ivy carried a large pot over to the table. "Dinner's ready. Actually, Finn, you can help. You can set the table." Her sassy grin came into play, momentarily striking him as mute as a junior high boy asked to talk about his feelings.

"What a privilege. Thank you." He stood and mock-bowed, and she laughed.

Ivy placed fresh buns on the table as he finished setting it along with a container of what looked to be whipped butter.

She waited until they'd prayed before lifting the lid from the covered dish.

He peered inside. Pot roast. It smelled and looked just

like his mom's—carrots and potatoes nestled against the browned beef.

"How did you— Is that my mom's recipe?"

Ivy nodded, obviously enjoying the moment. "I asked Charlie what your favorite meal was, and she went one step better and got me the recipe from your mom."

So that was why he'd recognized the scent.

"Ivy." Finn swallowed. "This is a really good surprise. Thank you."

"Though you were pretty terrible about not bugging me about it, weren't you?"

"I was pretty terrible. I had no idea that I couldn't handle a surprise until this week."

Her mouth curved to match his. "I realize we invaded your life living at the ranch." She handed him the large spoon. "I just wanted you to know that I see what you did for us, and I appreciate it."

"You're welcome." He'd thought that Ivy and the girls staying in the bunkhouse would be a drain on him by adding chaos to his life, but that really hadn't happened. Ivy had been a help, not a hindrance. Could he be wrong about staying out of her life in other ways, too? The sense of relief he felt at that possibility surprised him as much as her dinner had.

It wasn't until the girls finished eating and asked to be dismissed from the table that Finn had a chance to question Ivy about her day.

"So? What happened today?"

With her head down and her fork making race car patterns around the excess food still left on her plate, he would guess she hadn't heard him.

The fact that Ivy had barely eaten was a crime, because the meal was amazing.

"Are you going to eat anything or just stare at it?"

She glanced up, surprise scrawled across her features. "I'm eating." A half smile formed. "Sort of."

"I'm guessing whatever happened today has been on your mind all dinner."

"Sorry I haven't been great company."

"You were fine." Even without her carrying the conversation, Finn had still enjoyed the time with her and the girls.

"So what was it? Something with your parents?"

"Nope. Not them this time. It was your sister, actually."

Oh, boy. Did he want to hear this? Finn didn't care to get involved with anything between Charlie and Ivy.

She glanced at the triplets, making sure they were occupied, before continuing. "Charlie asked if I'd consider staying in Westbend to run the café."

Finn reeled as if twenty pounds of bricks had just landed on his bare feet. "She *what*?"

"Right? I was in shock. I am in shock. I instantly disregarded the idea, because it's impossible. Isn't it? But I also can't stop thinking about it."

He could understand that. This was huge.

"What am I supposed to do? How am I even supposed to process something like this? I'm *so* confused."

Finn set his fork down on top of his cleared plate. He'd had three helpings and was trying to resist a fourth. "If you stick around and it means more dinners for me, I'm going to need a personal trainer."

She waved a dismissing hand. "Please. You work it all off throwing around bales of hay or whatever you do out on the ranch."

Humor surfaced. "Speaking of the ranch, I once

promised the girls I'd take them out to feed the cattle, and I never followed through. Would Saturday work?"

"They would love that. That would be great. Thanks."

"Good. Now back to your dilemma."

Her groan spoke volumes.

"If you're this upset by the offer, that must mean you're at least a little bit interested. Right?"

She froze, then reluctantly nodded.

"All right. What are the benefits of moving to California?"

"My parents are well off. They'll make sure the girls have whatever they need. They'll pay for the best preschool, not that I'm even sure I want the girls to go there, but still. I'd have help. Everything wouldn't be just on me. The pressure to provide wouldn't be solely on me. My parents will likely hold it against me that I need the help, but at the same time, they'll provide it. Even if it does come with a guilt trip."

"And what are the benefits of staying in Westbend?"

"We'd get to build our own life." Did she know how her eyes perked with interest at that? "The girls would grow up in a small town. They'd have the freedom to play and be kids and mess up and get dirty and skin their knees. My mom has all kinds of lessons and things planned for them. The idea is suffocating. I keep telling her no, thank you, but she won't listen. I'm not sure if she thinks I'm refusing because of money, but I'm not. I just want the girls to have a relaxed childhood. They'll be in school long enough. Plenty will be required of them as they grow up. Is it so wrong to let them be kids right now?" Her voice fired up, heating, growing with determination as she delivered the last question.

"There's nothing wrong with that." Finn checked his

gut. Did he want Ivy to stay or go? He wasn't sure. He cared about her well-being and that of the girls. He had to wonder if staying in Colorado would be good for all of them. Certainly Ivy could do it—she could raise the triplets without her parents' assistance. And if she did, that would also mean she wouldn't have her parents' intrusion. But at the same time, her folks could certainly provide a higher level of living for them.

He was torn for her and with her. "I don't know what to tell you."

"You don't have any advice for me? A well-thought-out plan I can follow?"

"Unfortunately not." And even if he was leaning one way, he couldn't tell her that. He didn't want his opinion to sway her. It would be getting too involved. It would be too much like what had gone down with Chrissa. Ivy had to figure this out on her own.

But he could pray. "I don't have an answer, but I can pray for you to know what to do."

She inhaled deeply and let it out slowly. "That would be great. Thanks, Finn. And on the off chance we did decide to stay, we wouldn't live in the bunkhouse. I'd find something with a kitchen where we aren't invading your world."

And how lonely would that be? But she was right, of course. The bunkhouse wasn't a good long-term fit.

"I might not have answers for you, but I believe you'll know what to do. You have great instincts from what I've seen. You just need to trust them."

"I've beat myself up over having terrible instincts forever. Before Lee I would have agreed with you, but somewhere along the way I lost them like one of the girls trying to keep track of both gloves."

"Did you see red flags with Lee?"

"A year and a half ago, I would have told you no. But now that I've worked through so much, I'd say yes. They were there. I just didn't see them."

"Or you didn't want to see them."

"Exactly."

"It was the same with me and the woman in North Dakota. The signs were there. I just didn't want to read them."

"Well. That makes me feel better, because you seem like you have your life all together and figured out."

"That's definitely not the case. And for all that you've been through, Ivy, you're a champ. You make it look easy raising three girls, stopping to open a café when your car breaks down in the middle of a cross-country trip. Not a lot of people could handle what you have, and you've handled it well."

Her smile grew watery. "Thanks."

She's not the mess I once feared her to be. When Ivy had first arrived, Finn had jumped to conclusions based on circumstance. But he could see now that he'd been wrong all this time. Ivy was amazing. Life had handed her really hard things, but she'd done well with them. And besides the fact that she and the girls were staying in the bunkhouse—which Charlie had orchestrated— she'd never asked to be rescued. She'd always been careful to show him she appreciated using the space, even though it was unfinished. She didn't just take the way Chrissa had.

They spent the rest of the night talking and hanging out, eating the cupcakes he'd picked up from the bakery, the girls entertaining them, Ivy telling him stories about how she'd learned to love cooking and the crazy lessons her mom had signed her up for as a kid.

Compared to the date he'd been on this week, Ivy was so easy to be with.

How would he ever find anyone who remotely compared to her after she'd gone? And what if she stayed? Would that change things between them and allow him to pursue something with her? Before tonight, he would have said no.

But the revelation he'd had after dinner had shocked him into thinking possibly yes.

Chapter Eleven

Saturday dawned bright and chilly.

The girls were bundled in hats, gloves and winter jackets for their cattle feeding experience, and their excitement level was extreme. Last night Ivy had heard them whispering to each other long after she'd tucked them in. And though it had taken a minute to rouse them this morning, they were hyperawake now.

The four of them approached Finn outside the barn. The large flatbed truck was covered in the back with bales of hay. He rounded the vehicle and studied them.

"You sure about this? It's not as exciting as you might think."

The girls all nodded their heads.

"I wanna see the cows," Reese said quietly.

"I want to ride one!" Sage's demand made them laugh.

"Definitely can't do that." Ivy mussed her hair, then glanced at Finn. "We're ready. Back out now and we'll both experience the wrath of three meltdowns."

The skin around Finn's eyes crinkled. "Can't have that. Let's load up."

They piled into the truck, and Ivy used the seat belt

to lock the girls into place. Which left her in the middle next to Finn.

Their arms and jean-clad legs brushed against each other. Neither said anything about the contact, but an electrical current zipped through the cab. Finn's grip strangled the steering wheel, and his jaw went tight. Ivy wasn't sure if it was because he felt the same connection she did or because he was trying to avoid feeling anything.

Based on who he'd been when they'd first met, she'd have to go with the second.

The truck rumbled over the uneven terrain, and the girls giggled at the ride, talking about the mountain peaks that still held snow and how far the land went without houses or people.

If their old friends back in Connecticut could see them now, they'd accuse Ivy of turning into a country bumpkin, and they'd be right. She was consistently surprised by how much she enjoyed this land, the small town, the slower pace.

Even with the hectic work of opening the café, her evenings were calm and spent with her girls. Charlie didn't expect overtime out of her, and Ivy couldn't help but wonder what life in California would be like—what kind of job she would find and how long it would take to be successful enough to move her and the girls out of her parents' house. Years, most likely. She should be okay with that—and she was grateful her parents were willing to support them—but she also craved the freedom Westbend had provided for them.

She hadn't made a decision yet regarding Charlie's offer, nor did she know how to. She'd told Charlie she was still praying and thinking, and the woman had respected that, giving her time. But a conversation had to happen soon.

Ivy felt stuck between both worlds. The café opening was Wednesday night. She had originally planned to stay for one week after that. Now the future was as wide open as the land stretching in front of her, though far more confusing.

They reached the cattle and Finn put the truck in Park. "Usually Cliff would hop out and ride on the back, releasing hay as I drive. Or the other way around. You ready to drive?"

What? "No, I'm not going to drive this thing." Not only was the truck huge, she had no idea where to go and not run over something she shouldn't. Like a cow. Or wait… Were cattle different than cows? She considered asking Finn and then thought better of it. No need to flash her newbie card on repeat.

Finn chuckled. "Thought that might be your answer. Let's go." He was out the door before Ivy could move and showed up on the passenger side. He unloaded the girls, bringing them around to the flatbed and lifting them up. Ivy joined them.

Like a veteran, he checked what order the girls were in today. Once they volunteered that information, he showed them how to tear off a square of hay and helped each of them shove it from the platform.

Reese was precise in how she handled hers—gently pushing until it floated from the trailer. Sage kicked hers with a pent-up aggression that made Ivy wince and wonder where she'd gone wrong. But after, her smile was bright and blinding, so maybe Ivy was overthinking. Lola's turn was equal parts fascination and delight. The girls immediately began naming the cattle.

Finn's gaze twinkled as it met and held Ivy's. No words were needed. The beautiful morning and the land surrounding them was a testament to God's creation, and Ivy felt peace in the marrow of her bones.

I'm free.

Where had that thought come from? Like a dam that had broken open, Ivy's inner dialogue continued.

Look at your babies. They're amazing. They're living their best life in Westbend, loving time with Ms. Lina and feeding cattle and settling into this town as if they were always meant to be here.

I'm not trapped in a loveless marriage.

The accident didn't cause permanent damage to any of us.

The future is wide open. I'm free. The past doesn't have a hold on me anymore.

She lifted her arms, aligning her face with the sky. The last years of hardship fell away as the sun warmed the earth and her children giggled and found new ways to push hay from the truck and Finn let her just be in the moment. He didn't question her strange antics. Didn't force her back to reality.

Her arms switched to a self-hug as tears pooled and slipped down her cheeks. The moisture wasn't enough that the girls noticed. They were too enthralled with their current job. And Ivy was glad, because she didn't want to explain the emotion to them. She simply wanted to experience it. They weren't sad tears. They were tears of release.

Eventually, Finn hopped down from the truck and removed each of the girls. He loaded them back into the cab, then returned to offer her a hand.

She took it and leaped back to the ground.

"We need to move the truck." Finn held on to her hand after her descent, his concerned eyes asking questions his mouth didn't broach.

"I just figured out that I'm free. Everything that happened with Lee, even with all I've done to process it…it still had a hold on me. I forgot how to be me when I was married to him, and I think I just found myself again." She scanned their surroundings. "In the middle of this field." She laughed. "The girls were my only focus for so long, and they still are, but suddenly it's like a weight has been lifted. For the first time, I feel like I can make any decision and it's going to be okay. If we stay, great. If we go, great. I'm okay and the girls are going to be, too. Look how well they've done with our unexpected time in Westbend. That tells me they can survive my parents' house, or they can survive here or anywhere in between. God and I get to decide together. The freedom to make a decision and know either way it's going to be okay…that's everything to me."

Did Ivy have any idea how stunning she was right now? She glowed from the inside out. When she'd lifted her face to the sky, Finn's heart had raced so fast he'd had to latch onto a bale of hay to steady the earthquake she'd unknowingly created in him.

How could he have ever considered her or her life a mess?

Finn had never been more wrong about anything.

He swallowed twice to get his vocal cords functioning. "Good for you. There's nothing I want more for you than that freedom, and I have no doubt you'll be amazing whatever you decide." He squeezed Ivy's hand before letting go. He wasn't even sure she'd realized they were still touching.

"I wish Lee had believed in me like you do."

If she knew the way he'd only seen the messiness of her situation in the beginning, she would be so wounded. The idea that Finn had ever struggled to see Ivy instead of her circumstances embarrassed him. He'd been judgmental and prideful, and he prayed she would never know that side of him.

"I don't want to hold Lee responsible for how I disappeared during our marriage, because I'm the one who stopped being me. I'm the one who stopped having an opinion because it wasn't worth it. I'm the one who buried myself. There's no one else to blame."

"There's one other person to blame." Finn's skin heated with upset at the man who'd had Ivy's love and hadn't appreciated her.

"I know someone hurt you, Finn, but I hope you can move past it. I thought I had before, but now I'm realizing that part of it was still holding me captive."

She did look different. Her features had shed the worry and concern that had plagued her when he'd first met her. When she'd been fearful over her girls' safety. When she'd still been searching for herself.

She'd definitely been found.

"I think…I'm okay. I think I have moved on." When Ivy had left his house the other night after their dinner, Finn had found himself disappointed that things had stayed platonic. He'd wanted more with her after so long of avoiding exactly that.

And he'd known in that moment the difference between what he'd felt for Chrissa and what he now felt for Ivy. He'd been concerned for Chrissa, and in that process, he'd developed feelings for her. But what he'd started to feel for Ivy was completely different. He wasn't rescuing her like he'd feared he would end up doing. She was rescuing him by showing him what a balanced relationship looked like. By reminding him that just because something had happened in the past didn't mean it would happen in the future.

And yet, she could decide to leave, and there was nothing he could do to stop her. Nothing he *should* do to stop her. She'd worked so hard to gain her freedom. How could he be the one to disrupt that by asking her to stay?

He couldn't.

"I think the worst moment in my marriage was when Lee changed jobs. He didn't even tell me until after he'd made the decision and committed to the switch. That's when I realized how disconnected we were. I wanted to confront him about it, but do you know what I did instead?"

Finn shook his head.

"I threw him a congratulations dinner party and pretended I'd been on board the whole time. Pretended as if I'd known about the interview process, which had taken months. I was so mortified that he'd kept me out of the loop. And when I finally asked him about it later, he'd told me that he didn't think I cared what he was doing as long as the money came in." She sniffled. "I didn't care about money then, nor do I now. It was never about that. But I let him shame me with that, and after, I shut down even more. I just… Something in me died during our marriage. But I feel alive right now. Thanks to you." His heart grew ten sizes. "And Charlie. And everyone else in this town who's welcomed me and given me a chance."

"Everyone deserves a chance." *Especially you.* He wanted to tell her how amazing she was, how much he respected her and craved being with her, but Finn *couldn't* influence her future plans. Couldn't say anything that would push her in one direction or another.

This was her decision, and he refused to be another Lee in her life.

Ivy needed the space to work things out on her own, and just like he'd originally planned, Finn would give it to her.

Even if it killed him.

"Thank you for being the kind of friend who let me heal. When I arrived here, I didn't realize how far I had left to go."

"It wasn't as far as you think. And you've been that for me, too." He avoided using the word *friend*, because while she was that, she was more to him. Yes, he'd asked to be put in the friend category, but now that he wanted out of that well, it was too deep, the sides were too slippery, the effect on Ivy too great.

Pounding sounded from the truck. All three girls peered out the back window of the cab, their patience obviously expired. Lola stuck out her tongue while Sage had gone straight to exasperated with them, and Reese's lips wobbled like she was near tears.

Finn and Ivy's gazes collided with amusement.

"Oh, boy. We're in trouble now." Ivy waved at the girls. "We're coming! Hang on."

"We do need to finish feeding these cattle. You good to go? Or do you have any more revelations?"

Ivy rolled her eyes, but her mega smile was enough

to make him stumble as they walked to the cab. "I'm ready."

"Why have you been talking back there for hours and hours?" Sage questioned when they opened the driver's door, making them both laugh. "The cows are hungry."

Ivy buckled the girls again, not sure how far they'd be moving. "Wait—are they called cows or cattle?"

"Cattle refers to all of them. Only the females are called cows. Heifers are young females who haven't given birth yet."

Ivy grimaced. "I feel like that's something I should have learned in kindergarten. I just— Never mind. You wouldn't understand."

"I understand your city is showing."

Ivy's face wreathed with amusement and sunshine. "You, Finn Brightwood, don't understand a thing."

She couldn't be closer to the truth, because Finn definitely didn't understand why God would bring Ivy and the girls into his life when he couldn't do anything to keep them there.

Chapter Twelve

Finn's reaction to being around Ivy had gone from avoidance to eagerness to straight-up pain.

In the days since they'd taken the girls to feed the cattle and he'd finally admitted his feelings for Ivy to himself, they'd been multiplying like germs in a petri dish.

Which was why he was dreading the opening night of the café.

He should be happy for his sister and for Ivy. For what they'd accomplished. But all he could think about was Ivy leaving. She hadn't told him if she'd made up her mind regarding staying or going, and he hadn't asked.

He was planning on her leaving next week like she'd originally intended. Not hoping they'd stay was easier. That way, if they didn't, he'd handle it. Somehow.

Finn exited his truck and walked the short distance to the café. He'd parked farther away to allow room for others to park closer. The soft opening would surely draw a crowd, especially with Charlie's addition of the auction.

Finn had tried to tell her no. He really had. But he'd lost that battle miserably, and his boots were heavy with the knowledge that he was being auctioned off tonight like...cattle. How ironic.

He'd worn his usual for the event jeans, boots and a light blue button-down untucked that Charlie had once told him looked good with his complexion, whatever that meant. He'd wondered for about two seconds if he was supposed to dress up, and then had decided that he didn't care. His usual would have to do.

The door jingled as he opened it, and five expectant faces swung his way. Ryker, Charlie, Ivy, Kaia and George. He'd met Kaia in passing at church, but George he didn't know.

Charlie waved a dismissing hand. "Oh, I thought you were our first guest."

"I am."

"You're my brother! You don't count."

"Ouch." Finn moved the flowers he'd brought to his left hand and greeted Ryker with a handshake.

"Don't worry. She said the same thing about me."

Charlie squawked. "You both matter. You both know that's not what I meant."

They exchanged grins.

Ryker frowned at the flowers. "Really? You showing me up, Brightwood?"

Finn raised a shoulder. "It's what I do."

He greeted Kaia, introduced himself to George and then handed one bunch of flowers off to Ivy and one to Charlie.

His sister slugged him on the arm. "Finn! This is so nice. Thank you. I need to find something to put these in." She scooted behind the counter.

Ivy's response was harder to read. She looked from the flowers to him with wonder and confusion. "What are these for?"

He motioned to the café. "This. You did this with Charlie. You deserve to celebrate and be celebrated."

Her eyes softened. "Thank you. I love flowers."

"Good." For a minute there he'd thought he was in trouble for bringing them—and not just from Ryker.

"I can't get them to stand up because this mug is too short," Charlie said from behind the register. "I think I'm going to have to run upstairs to my apartment and grab some vases."

"I'll go." Ryker's response was dry and agitated with a side of humor. "Thanks a lot, man." He shoved Finn as he went by.

"What? I can't help it that you've failed as a boyfriend."

Ryker's laughter could be heard echoing down the hallway to the back door.

Now that his hands were free, Finn felt out of place. "Can I help with anything? How's the setup going?"

"Yes." Charlie pointed to the sign and string on the counter. "We still need to hang the charity's sign. I want it over there, right by the raised stage area."

The wooden platform wasn't much, but Finn imagined that was where the cattle—like him—would stand on the auction block.

"It's like hammering a nail in my own coffin."

Charlie chuckled. "Sorry, brother!"

She wasn't sorry. She was glowing with sibling victory.

He got to work hanging the sign, and Ivy came over

to evaluate after he'd finished. "The right side is lower than the left."

Finn stepped back to analyze. "No, it's not."

Her mouth curved. "It's not."

"Ah. So you're just having fun with me." Last time he'd seen her at the café, she'd been none too happy with him because of their almost kiss and his response to it. If only he could go back and have that conversation—and that opportunity—again. He'd do it differently, that was for sure. Ivy's mind must have followed the same path as his, because her vision bounced from his lips as if they were on fire and she was kindling.

"The place looks great, doesn't it?"

"It does." Although he was far more interested in studying her than Charlie's Pit Stop. She wore the same casual burgundy dress she'd worn the night of the cattle men's dinner. Back then he'd thought her pretty. Now he knew she was beautiful inside and out. "What's on the agenda for tonight?"

"From what I've heard, you are."

He groaned. "Charlie told you she forced me into doing the auction?"

Ivy's laugh was light. "Yep, and I can't wait to see it."

"That's just cruel."

"Don't worry, Finn. You'll be a hot commodity. You won't get left standing up there."

He wanted to dissect exactly what she'd meant by *hot*, but his brain was firing with too much upset. "I hadn't even thought about having to stand up front while no one bids on me. Great. Now I'm going to be sweating bullets."

Ivy laughed again.

"You're finding this a little too amusing."

"I really am. I can't help it. I'm nervous over tonight, so I'm finding distractions any way I can. And you're one of them."

"I'll happily be a distraction for you." The moment the words slipped out Finn knew he'd gone too far.

Ivy's eyes went as wide as oversize coffee mugs, and her mouth formed the cutest little O. He'd told himself that he'd stay out of her business and decisions, and that meant not letting her know he was growing attached to her. That she was burrowing into his heart and creating a space no one but her could fill.

And yet, here he was, flirting with her.

If he couldn't fight for Ivy, then maybe Finn could at least appreciate being with her this evening. He could give himself that extension of the rules he'd set, couldn't he? And time with her would give him the strength to survive the auction.

Because he didn't expect to enjoy that part at all.

Ivy made a latte behind the counter and served it to Alma Dinnerson, a quirky woman whose style had gotten stuck in the seventies on a train of polyester. But despite her interesting fashion choices that Lola would take issue with, Alma obviously had quite the business sense, because she was Kaia and Ryker's landlord and also owned other real estate in town, according to Charlie.

When Alma moved away from the counter, Ivy's vision landed on Finn and stuck like Gorilla Glue. From his conversation across the room, he must have sensed her attention, because his mouth gave the slightest lift.

Ivy's stomach mimicked the movement as she focused on another patron's order.

She and Finn had been careful to keep things platonic since the night of their almost kiss, which was smart. But she wasn't sure she could say they were acting the definition of that word tonight. And she also couldn't deny she was enjoying Finn's attention.

As Ivy handed the next coffee across the counter, Finn approached with a stack of dirty dishes.

"Where do you want all of this?"

Ivy reached for it. "I'll take it. Sorry. You shouldn't have to be helping out."

"What else am I going to do with myself?"

She sorted the silverware and plates into the dish tub, then tossed the paper products. "Mingle. Talk. Seems you know most of the people in this place, and yet you've only lived in town since fall."

"It's a small town, and I did live at Wilder Ranch for a stint a few years back. Have you met the Wilder clan?" He pointed to a group of couples. One of the women—Mackenzie, if Ivy had her facts straight—was holding a newborn baby. Her husband stole the little one from her, obviously enamored with both of them, and Ivy's heart fluttered at the picture they made. What she wouldn't give to hold that baby for a couple minutes, especially since she'd likely never have that experience again. Everything had gone by so fast when the girls were babies. She'd been in survival mode. It would be nice to rewind to that time and have the bandwidth to enjoy it more.

"No, I've heard of them. Seen them at church. Haven't been introduced."

"I'll introduce you tonight. Luc, Gage and Jace all attend my men's Bible study. Luc's a Wilder, and Gage and Jace both married Wilder sisters."

Were introductions necessary? She was leaving with the girls next week. Wasn't she?

Today she'd told Charlie that she would give her a decision tomorrow. Ivy had been holding out, hoping an answer would come to her. It hadn't yet. It probably wouldn't overnight, either. Which meant she'd just have to trust her gut—the one she'd doubted for so many years—and choose.

No wrong answer, remember? Either way we'll make it work.

Ivy still felt peace and freedom, but that didn't mean she'd been hit over the head with an exact plan of what to do.

"You okay?" Finn squeezed her arm, his fingers lingering against her skin, heating the spot as if the sun had seared her.

"I will be. Just thinking about decisions that need to be made." And this evening wasn't helping anything. The vibe in Westbend was so welcoming and the café so near and dear to her in such a short amount of time. All of it was swaying her toward staying. These people— especially the man studying her with tender concern— were pulling her in.

Somewhere along the way things had shifted between her and Finn. Ivy felt the earth moving under her feet and wasn't sure how to adjust her balance. Did she lean toward him…or away? Was he really who he said he was? Or was she missing something, like she had with Lee?

"Ivy, I wish—" Finn swallowed, his Adam's apple bobbing.

"Excuse me, I'm here for the auction but I'm running late. Where do I register?" The young man who'd sidled up next to Finn across the counter from Ivy had a Clark Kent vibe. Dark-framed glasses. Espresso-colored hair parted on one side.

"I'll talk to you later." Finn slipped away.

Kaia must have gathered that Ivy's tongue or brain or whole nervous system wasn't functioning, because she swept in to answer the new arrival.

"Right here." She pointed to the clipboard. "Was your name already on the list?"

"Yes. Charlie contacted me and asked if I'd be willing. And since I was a foster kid until my parents adopted me at age two, I couldn't really say no."

Kaia smiled, and the man noticed, though she had no idea she was gaining any attention, since her concentration was on the sheet.

She traced down the list with her finger. "You must be Maxwell. That's the only name left."

"Just Max."

Kaia introduced herself, and Ivy feigned busyness while covertly watching the two of them interact.

Max was listening to Kaia explain how the auction would work, with interest that was focused not on her speech, but on *her*. And Kaia was still completely oblivious.

"Will you be bidding tonight?" Max's cheeks reddened at his blatant inquiry.

"No, the staff is staying out of the auction. We're leaving that to the guests."

His expression morphed from hope to disappointment in a millisecond. "Right. That makes sense. Well, thank you for the help, Kaia." He eased into the crowd.

"Poor guy." Ivy wiped the front counter, the smell

of bleach wafting from the rag. "I don't think he's very comfortable with the auction."

"Right? His introversion was coming out his pores." Kaia's pretty features softened with empathy.

"The good news is the auction is starting in ten minutes, so he won't have to mingle long."

The two of them handled a rush of drink orders while George plated appetizers that were complimentary and continued serving them. Charlie flitted about behind the counter, chatting with the guests, checking on the sound system for the auction.

The turnout was excellent. No doubt Charlie was raising awareness for her business along with funds for the foster charity. Win-win.

A whistle sounded, and Charlie climbed up on a chair at the front of the room to garner everyone's attention.

"Hello." She adjusted the microphone so it was closer to her mouth. "Thank you for being here to celebrate the opening with us and thank you for supporting Kids' Keepers. This is an amazing charity that provides physical items for foster children, and I'm so glad that the proceeds from tonight's auction will be going to them. Our auctioneer this evening will be Ryker Hayes." Charlie motioned to Ryker, who was standing next to her. "So, without further ado, let's bring out our first bachelor and get started!"

The women in the room gave a collective cheer, and Kaia and Ivy shared an amused glance. As Kaia had told Max, neither of them had registered for bidding because, one, they were employees of the café, and two, neither wanted anything to do with snatching up a man at the moment.

Kaia had told Ivy as they'd been working and training together that she was focused on Honor. Ivy understood the sentiment, since her girls were her first priority.

Two men were quickly placed on the auction block—which was a small raised platform—and awarded to the highest bidder. Max was third in line and looked as pleased as a kid who'd been told he had to go to bed early while his friends got to stay up and play. Ivy felt for him before the bidding even started.

Ryker read his bio. "Maxwell is a computer programmer who built his first computer at eleven years old." Someone whistled. "He's twenty-six and hopes to marry himself off before his mom manages to do it." Laughter followed.

The bidding started out fast, but it was quickly clear that one woman was determined to win time with Max—sweet, quirky, fiftysomething-year-old Alma Dinnerson.

Alma raised her paddle to increase her bid. "I need computer help." Some people chuckled. "And my phone is doing something weird, too."

Ivy groaned. "Oh, no. Poor Max." His ears joined his cheeks, the bright crimson visible from her and Kaia's perch behind the counter. Was it worse not to be bid on at all? Or to be bid on by Alma?

Kaia's breath leaked out, and she lunged for the pen and clipboard on the counter that held the women's names. She scribbled hers and took the next number, quickly lifting the paddle into the air.

"We've got a battle on our hands," Ryker called out, hamming up his time on the microphone. "Remember ladies, not only is this handsome young lad single, he comes with technological skills that can't be beat. Don't let him pass you by."

Ivy nudged Kaia, her voice low. "He's cute."

"I'm not bidding on him because of that. I just… He was sweet to sign up. And you know Charlie probably forced him to."

"Yep. And he's cute."

"He's really not my type."

"What is your type?"

"No job, awful decision-maker, short temper." Kaia winced.

"So maybe he's not a terrible option." Both of them murmured the phrase at the same time.

After a few bids back and forth, Alma must have decided she wasn't going to beat out Kaia, because she bowed out. Once Kaia was declared the winner, Max removed himself from the platform lightning-fast, obviously ready to be anywhere but in front of the crowd.

But then, after taking a few steps, he stopped. "Alma, I'll still help you with whatever computer need you have. No purchase necessary."

The crowd roared with approval.

As Max made his way toward Kaia, people parted, some slapping him on the back, others congratulating him.

Ivy made herself busy wiping the table nearest to the counter so that she could give Kaia and Max space… and still overhear, of course.

"Thanks for rescuing me up there." Even the man's voice had an endearing quality. Not needy. Not whiny. Just low and calm and strangely resigned.

"Of course."

"And don't worry. I won't make you follow through on the date or whatever it is we're supposed to do. I know you were just throwing me a lifeline."

Ah. Now the resignation made sense. Max didn't deem himself to be in Kaia's league. His professor-like vibe could be a turnoff for some, but Ivy found it appealing. Surely Kaia could see how quality Max was.

"I appreciate that, actually, because I wasn't really planning to date anyone right now. I just gained back custody of my daughter, and I'm really focusing on her. And bettering myself."

Knife in the heart! Ivy's palm rested over her chest.

"I understand." After thanking Kaia again, Max made his way toward Alma, likely to get her contact information in order to help with her technology needs.

"You're not just going to let him go like that, are you?"

Kaia busied herself by restacking cups that were already stacked. "He wasn't really wanting to go out with me. He just came because of the charity."

"Kaia, the man was looking at you like he was dying of thirst and you were the only water source left in town. I get it if you don't want to date or he isn't your type, but shouldn't you give him a chance?"

Kaia bit her lip as Max made his way to the door. He must have exchanged information with Alma, because he was making his escape.

The younger woman groaned and rounded the counter. She caught up to Max just as he neared the exit. By the way he lit up, Kaia was imparting good news.

Ivy swung her hips in a little happy dance, silently celebrating them. She understood Kaia putting Honor first, but she also didn't want her to miss out on a great guy like Max because of fearing she'd repeat the past.

The similarities to her own situation with Finn walloped Ivy like a slap to the face.

Good thing she didn't have any time to process *that* right now. Yes, it was a good thing she was busy working and that Ms. Lina was planning to drop off the girls any second. Because if Ivy traveled down the what-if road with Finn, she wasn't sure how she'd ever merge back onto reality lane.

Chapter Thirteen

Finn was desperate for help, and the only person he could think of to rescue him would stomp on his foot if she knew why he was asking.

But since he had only two options—upsetting Ivy, or enduring another date with the woman from last week—he'd pick door number one...and hopefully survive to talk about it.

Ivy was so busy watching Kaia converse with the man she'd bid on by the front door of the café that she didn't notice him approach her.

He called her name twice before she whirled in his direction.

"Oh, hey. What's up?"

"I'm desperate. I need help."

Her eyes narrowed. "What kind of help?"

Admitting he'd gotten himself into a sticky situation was as cringeworthy as stepping in a pile of manure.

"There's a woman here who I've gone out with." Once. Last week. Not that he planned to share the details of that stupid decision. "She says she's going to bid on me, and I just..." It would be terrible if she did. Finn didn't have any remaining interest in Bethany. He only wanted one woman, but she was off-limits.

He could wait and hope that someone like Alma who needed help with manual labor would bid on him, but he couldn't risk it. Bethany had confessed when she'd arrived that she planned to bid on him. He could attempt to reiterate to her again that he wasn't interested, but he'd already done that once, and it obviously hadn't worked.

After their coffee date, Finn had gently relayed to Bethany that he didn't feel a connection. It had been hard, but he'd been up-front.

She wasn't listening.

Saying it again would just be painful for both of them.

Ivy motioned to the front door, where Lina had just entered with the triplets. "The girls are here. I need to grab them."

Finn was up for bidding next, and his skin was starting to crawl at the lack of control he'd have once he stepped onto that platform. Stinking Charlie. How did she talk him into this stuff?

After Ivy greeted Lina and the girls and the older woman left, she faced him again. The triplets, at least, were happy to see him…and Finn wasn't above using that to his advantage.

"Girls, I need you to do me a favor. Hang on." He hurried over to the counter, filled out a slot for bidding and took a paddle with the next number on it. He returned to the four of them. By Ivy's half-amused, half-exasperated sigh, she knew what he was up to.

And because she would have to orchestrate it, he held her gaze while he pitched the girls his idea.

"When I'm up there, I need you girls to bid on me, okay? Your mom will help you know when." *Please?*

He waited, not above pleading, until Ivy gave a slight nod. *Yes.*

Finn took a hundred-dollar bill from his wallet. Surely bidding wouldn't reach that amount. He handed it to Lola.

Ivy snorted. "You're crazy, Finn Brightwood. Here—" She held out her hand. "Let me hold it, Lo. I'll keep track of it."

Lola's fist tightened around the money, but the I-don't-think-so mom look Ivy shot her had her reluctantly forking it over.

"I want to hold the paddle first." Sage lunged for it, then Reese. It slipped from Finn's grip and the triplets engaged in a tug-of-war when Lola joined in.

"Hold on, hold on." Finn snagged it back from them. Ivy would never forgive him if the girls threw down in a crowd like this. And he'd been foolish not to check who was first today. "This works just like everything else. Whose day is it?"

"Mine!" Reese raised her hand.

"Okay, Reese, you're first. Who's next?"

"Me." Lola tossed Sage a sassy, victorious glance, her little arms crossing over her stylish yellow shirt. She looked like a model for a children's store, with her cuffed jeans and ankle boots.

"You don't have to be so mean about it," Sage huffed.

They knew the rules, so while they might not be happy about it, no one argued. "God bless Ivy for coming up with the rotating order."

She laughed. "You're welcome. Girls—" her attention switched to them "—there are some games and coloring pages over in the kids' corner. Go check it out."

They scooted across the room, dodging between adults.

"I'm up next. I should go up there."

Ivy's teeth pressed into her lip.

"What?"

"It's just…you haven't been in town that long. I didn't realize you'd dated anyone." Was she jealous? What Finn wouldn't give to find out.

"It was…recent. But only one date. It was nothing, really."

"I thought you said you weren't dating anyone because of what happened in North Dakota. I didn't realize… It's none of my business anyway. Never mind."

I'd be just fine if it was your business, but I can't do that. Not after he'd watched her celebrate her independence. Not after the stories she'd told him about Lee.

Her hand snaked up and tucked back a piece of her hair. She looked so pretty—always did. But he never told her so because of all the reasons not to.

"You look beautiful tonight, Ivy."

Surprise registered. "Thank you."

I've changed my mind about our previous discussion. No. It would be selfish of him to have that conversation. She had to be close to deciding whether she and the girls were going to stay in Westbend or continue on to California. Hadn't she told him over and over again how she'd lost herself in her marriage? He couldn't attempt to influence her. He just couldn't. And that was if she'd even consider dating him an option. She'd said no in their previous discussion.

"Sounds like the bidding is done. I'd better go." He tore himself away from her while wondering if he'd have to do the same next week…for good.

* * *

If Ivy didn't have money from Finn burning a hole in her pocket and the way he'd pleaded for rescue playing on repeat in her mind, she wouldn't be watching him stand on the auction platform at all.

She simply couldn't have endured witnessing another woman bidding on him, winning time with him. Couldn't have handled the thought of him almost kissing— or actually kissing—someone else. Somewhere along the way, she'd lost a chunk of her heart to Finn Brightwood. Unwise? Sure. But it had happened, nonetheless.

The question was, what was she going to do about it?

At the moment? Nothing.

She had other things to concentrate on, and figuring out the next step for her and the girls was higher on her priority list than dissecting her feelings for Finn.

The bidding started, and of course numerous women raised their paddles. Including one who looked like a teapot ready to steam.

She must be the woman he was avoiding. Why? Based on her looks, Ivy would say they were a match or at least in the same league. Who knew why Finn had gone out with her or why he didn't want to again?

Not your business, Ivy Darling. And yet, he somehow felt like hers.

Finn coughed, then shot her a panicked look.

She'd forgotten to have the girls bid. She raced over to the kids' corner and grabbed Reese, plunking her feet onto a chair.

"Going once," Ryker called out.

Ivy helped Reese lift the paddle into the air.

"Going twice—oh, wait, we have a new bidder. She

looks like a demanding one, Finn. You're going to have your hands full."

The crowd laughed.

The other woman bid again.

Ivy quickly pulled up another chair, situating Sage and Lola on it. She put the paddle in Lola's hand and helped her wave it when Ryker checked for their next bid. She should have had the girls prepared to bid instead of being lost in her own thoughts.

They went back and forth a few times. After Lola lifted the paddle again at Ivy's nudging, the other woman paused. Ivy's pulse roared in her ears. They were almost to the limit of the money Finn had given her.

The bidding continued and hit the hundred-dollar mark. Only Finn. No one else's bids had gone so high. Of course his would.

Whistles and applause came from the crowd. The bid was back to Ivy and the girls. She would have to break the barrier and go over the amount allotted, or they would lose Finn.

She motioned for Sage to raise the paddle. Keeping her fingers firmly lodged in her mouth, Sage used her other hand to bid. The crowd cheered. Some people teased the girls, encouraging them. Ivy didn't look away from Finn. She couldn't. Their gazes were fused to one another. The chatter of the room faded, and she only saw him. The questions vibrating from the marrow of her bones were reflected on his features. *Why?* She lifted one shoulder in answer because she couldn't give him more. Couldn't tell him that she wasn't sure she'd survive seeing him with another woman. How could she admit that when she was still torn over leaving or staying?

"Going once, going twice… *Sold* to the trio in the back!" Ryker called. The girls figured out they'd won and threw their arms in the air, engaging in their favorite celebration dance. Lola got knocked from the chair she was sharing with Sage just as Finn threaded through the crowd and reached them. He caught her midfall.

"You okay?" He set her on her feet.

"We won, Mista Finn. We won." Lola paused to peer up at him. "What did we win?"

"Me."

Her hands landed on her hips. "But we didn't need to win you. We already have you."

"That you do, Lola." Finn ruffled her hair, his focus on Ivy, much like it had been when she'd upped the bidding beyond the money he'd given her. "That you do."

Finn spent the remainder of the auction receiving congratulations and being teased about keeping up with the three girls who'd won his time and attention. At the end of the auction, Charlie thanked everyone for their donations and for celebrating the opening of the café.

Ryker stole the microphone from her. "I'd also like to celebrate this amazing woman who's now opened a second business in Westbend."

Whoops and cheers sounded.

"If you know Charlie, you know she's not frivolous, she cares deeply for everyone around her, and she is nothing if not practical. She once told me she wouldn't wear a wedding ring as a mechanic." A gasp threaded through the room. "So I've come up with a different solution." Ryker held up a photo of a ring tattoo. From

Finn's place at the back of the room, he couldn't see the detail, but Charlie's hand snaked up to cover her mouth.

"I love it." Her awed response carried over the now quiet crowd.

"Got it designed just for you." Everyone collectively strained to hear as the microphone slacked in Ryker's grip. "Charlotte Joy Brightwood, will you marry me?"

Her head began bobbing before her "Yes!" caused a roar of approval to sweep the room. Charlie crashed into Ryker, and he spun her around in a circle before depositing her feet back on the floor.

After that there was kissing. Finn wrinkled his nose. He could be happy for them, but he still didn't need to witness his sister locking lips.

It took him about fifteen minutes to make it up to the front to offer Charlie and Ryker congratulations since so many were doing the same.

He hugged Charlie. "Congratulations, sis."

"Thank you!" Her smile was huge. "Did you see it?" She shoved the picture at him. The design was intricate, made to mimic a wedding band, and it definitely fit her sense of logic in not wearing a ring while working on cars. So very Charlie. And well done of Ryker to know her that well.

"It's great. Very unique."

"Isn't it? I would never have thought of the idea, but I love it." Her happy sigh spoke volumes.

Finn shook Ryker's hand, slapping him on the back in congratulations. "Now I definitely didn't show you up with some grocery store flowers."

Ryker laughed. "Sorry I didn't tell you. I did talk to your dad. I'm guessing he kept it from you?"

"He sure did."

"I wasn't sure you could keep anything from your sister, so that was probably for the best."

It was true—he and Charlie were close. And that rift that North Dakota had placed between them had begun to heal when he'd had lunch with Charlie after church on Sunday and finally opened up about what had happened while he was there.

If Ivy could process her much harder scenario so well, Finn had determined to do the same. To be as strong as her.

His first step had been to share with his sister about what had gone on with Chrissa. She'd been understanding, of course. What else had he expected? And then she'd encouraged him to stay open and trust God for healing in all of it.

They'd moved on to other topics of conversation as if what he'd been through was normal, as if he was normal and hadn't failed miserably at saving Chrissa.

It had been restorative for him.

More people came by to congratulate Ryker and Charlie, so Finn got out of the way. He could talk to them later.

It was seven o'clock. Things had gone smoothly, and now people were filtering out of the café. He found Ivy, Kaia and George bustling around, sorting dirty dishes and tossing paper products. Wiping down counters. Sweeping floors in the areas that had emptied.

In order to be a help, Finn grabbed items as he made his way to the counter and past Ivy, depositing them in the dish bin.

"So," he asked her, "what do you plan to do with me now that you've won me?"

"I didn't win you, actually."

Charlie appeared, setting the clipboard and information from the winning bidders on the counter. "It's true. Technically the triplets won you." She pointed to the list. "Says their names right here."

Ivy checked her watch. "The way I see it, we have an hour or less of cleanup here."

Charlie nodded in agreement when Ivy glanced at her for confirmation.

"It's seven, which means the girls aren't at their bedtime yet. Which means you can take them out for ice cream." Ivy beamed. No doubt the idea had taken root the minute he forced the girls—and her—into bidding on him. She'd likely been waiting impatiently since they'd won, for the opportunity to deliver her verdict.

Charlie hooted. "You earned yourself a babysitting gig, Finn."

His stomach dropped to his boots. He wanted time with Ivy, too, but he couldn't exactly say that, could he?

"All right. Ice cream it is. Want me to help clean up? Or take them now?"

Ivy softened. "Actually, taking them now would be more helpful than cleaning up. That way they're entertained. And then you can cross your duty off your list. Especially since you gave us the money to bid on you."

"All the more reason that I owe you one. You saved me." Charlie was saying goodbye to a few remaining people, so Finn broached the question on his mind. "Why did you up the bid?"

"Why did you need saving?"

She deserved an answer, especially after their we-can't-date conversation, so he gave her what he could.

"Because I'm an idiot."

Her mouth curved reluctantly at that. It wasn't enough to explain himself, but it was all he had to give.

"I upped it because it was a good cause…and because it seemed you needed us for some reason."

"I did." *I do.* "Well, thank you."

She gave a hesitant nod. "You're welcome."

"Do you want me to bring the girls back to the bunkhouse after? I can have them start their bedtime routine so they're at least partially ready when you get there."

"You don't have to do that."

"I did make you bid on me when you didn't want to be involved."

"True." She shrugged as if accepting. "That would be amazing, actually. Lina put their car seats in my car. It's unlocked."

"Done. I'll text you when we're headed home." *Home.* That made it sound like they were together when of course they weren't. But what if they could be in the future?

Only Ivy could answer that. Only she could tell him if she planned to stay in Westbend or not. And tonight, when she came back to the ranch, maybe he'd scrounge up the nerve to ask her.

And maybe he'd survive her answer, too.

Chapter Fourteen

George and Kaia had walked out to their vehicles together, leaving Charlie and Ivy in the now quiet space. There wasn't much left to do. Just restock for tomorrow, since the café would be officially open, turn down the lights and lock up.

Would anyone show up? Would they be slammed or slow? Would Ivy know how to run everything? And how would Kaia do on her first shift? She'd been great tonight—attentive and hardworking but on the quiet side. George, on the other hand, was an outgoing personality, talkative, friendly. Between the two of them and Charlie, Ivy prayed the business would be a success.

When she considered the fact that she still wasn't sure if she planned to stay in Westbend or not, she was strangely nervous about the success of the café.

But then, Charlie had allowed her to take ownership, to make decisions and pour her heart and soul into this little place. If she did follow through on her plans to move to her parents', she would miss the freedom and success the café had provided for her.

And the people, too. Especially one dashing rancher

who had ignited ever-so-strong feelings in her tonight. Would leaving Finn behind in Colorado hurt as much as Ivy imagined it would?

"The last time I saw my brother flirt was in high school." Charlie's comment was a scary reflection of Ivy's thoughts, and she froze in the middle of restocking the to-go coffee cups. "Until tonight."

"You mean with the other woman? The one he went on a date with?"

Charlie snorted. "No. I mean with you. He's falling for you. And if you think I put him up to that in order to help my case of you staying in town, I did not."

Ivy laughed as her chest constricted with confusion and hope and fear.

"Even I would find that going too far. He definitely figured out how to feel about you all on his own."

Then why had he gone out with someone else? They'd decided not to get romantically involved, but that hadn't kept her heart from leaning heavily in Finn's direction.

"My first impression of Finn wasn't the most flattering."

"I can understand that." Charlie tossed the dirty dishrags from tonight into a small laundry basket she'd brought down from her apartment. "And now?"

"I can't help but wonder if he's real. Which person is he? The first or the second? Or some version in between?"

"That's a valid point. Before…" Charlie paused as if choosing her words. "He was different, before a situation that happened. And he's been slowly coming back to life since then, I think."

"You mean because of the woman in North Dakota?"

Charlie's wide eyes relayed her surprise. "He told you about Chrissa?"

Ivy nodded.

Her expression relaxed. "Well, that's good. Then I don't have to worry about saying too much if you know what happened. I can't stand how she played him, going all damsel-in-distress, dragging him into her chaos and then dropping him the moment he was out of sight. He should never have gotten involved with her in the first place, but that's Finn—good to the core. Always seeing the best in people. Always trying to save people and enter into their mess with them."

Ivy's blood turned to ice in her veins. *Always trying to save people and enter into their mess with them. Damsel in distress. Dragging him into her chaos.*

So…it wasn't just hurt that had kept Finn from pursuing anything romantic with Ivy. It was that she was a mess, too. He hadn't wanted to repeat his last mistake with a disaster like her. Someone whose life was in shambles and being rebuilt. Someone who'd had a liar and a coward for a husband. Someone who was raising triplets by herself. Someone who'd managed to slide off the road while driving cross-country in order to be rescued by her parents.

When you put it that way, no one would want to get involved with you, Ivy. True, and yet, the wound was so deep, so raw, that it consumed her skin, instantly heating her body to flu temperatures.

Since Charlie was looking at her with expectation, Ivy forced an answer. "Right." She swallowed the fiery ball clogging her throat. "Poor Finn getting taken in like that."

Despite her opposite intentions, Charlie had just un-

knowingly proven who Finn *really* was…and confirmed
that Ivy's intuition was still on hiatus, where it must
plan to remain her entire life.

How could she have been so wrong yet again?

Ivy finished restocking cups, trying with everything
in her not to let Charlie in on the fact that she'd been
privy to only a portion of that backstory.

"I think we're good to take off."

"Great." Ivy opened the cupboard that housed her
purse and clutched it against her chest as if it were a
shield that could erase the damage from the past few
minutes.

"Don't forget your flowers."

"I'm going to leave them here if that's okay with
you. There's no space for them at the bunkhouse." Ivy
couldn't even look at Finn's gift right now, let alone
touch it.

"Of course." Charlie checked the front door to confirm it was locked, and then they both walked toward
the back exit.

The woman paused with her hand on the light switch.
"Tonight went really great, Ivy. I couldn't have done it
without you. I know you said you'd let me know if you're
leaving or staying tomorrow, and I promised myself I
wouldn't pressure you, but…I'm really hoping for the
second option. In case you need any encouragement, I
just want you to know that."

It felt good to be wanted. Needed. "Thank you. I've
thought of little else since you broached the idea. Every
day I think I'm going to wake up and *know*. That the
decision will be clear." Her sigh echoed down to her
flats. "I guess that means I'm just going to have to de-

cide. That I'm not going to be hit over the head with what to do."

"I can hit you over the head if you want."

Ivy laughed. "I appreciate the offer, but I obviously just need to make a decision. It's so hard to know if I'm focusing on my own wants or what the girls need. And are those the same or different? That's what has me stuck."

"That certainly adds pressure. I hate to be the one pushing you. I do understand if you stick to your original plan, Ivy. And I don't regret hiring you for one second. If you were just here for a short time, then I'm thankful for that."

"Thank you for understanding. And appreciating me. I forgot what it felt like to be valuable for a while."

Charlie squeezed her arm before flipping off the lights and locking the door behind them.

Ivy tucked her sweater closer around her as she hurried to her vehicle. She scrambled into the driver's seat and started it to appease Charlie, who was waiting on the landing to her apartment to make sure she was safe.

She waved, and Charlie let herself into her apartment.

Ivy drove out of the lot and down the street until Charlie and the café and the mechanic shop faded from view. When her vision blurred with tears, she pulled to the side of the road and put the vehicle in Park.

"So when he said he couldn't kiss me, couldn't go there with me, it was never about another woman hurting him. It was about me and my life being a mess and him refusing to get involved. Ouch."

Her vehicle answered her with silence, and a gaping hole opened inside of her. Hadn't she been afraid of this very thing? That she couldn't trust her instincts. That she couldn't fall for Finn because it was too fast. That she didn't know the real him.

Ivy had just repeated all of the ways she'd failed with Lee…and somehow it hurt even more the second time around.

On the drive back to the ranch, Finn had cooked up a plan.

If he could get the girls in bed and maybe even asleep before Ivy got home, then he'd have her to himself. And despite his reservations over influencing her in any way, there was nothing he wanted more.

"Teeth brushed?" He stood by the bathroom door and observed the chaos of the three pajama-clad girls sharing the small space.

"I did mine already." Sage scooted by him and rushed into the living room.

Reese paused from brushing rather carefully for a three-year-old. "No, you didn't!"

"Hold on." Before Lola could chime in with her opinion and start World War III, Finn checked the toothbrush on the vanity. "It's dry." He raised his voice and stepped back so that Sage could hear him as she ran laps around the coffee table. "Which means you didn't brush, Sage. Come on. Come over here and get it done."

"No." Sage paused on the other side of the coffee table like an animal ready to bolt, her sassy mug shouting, *You're not in charge of me.*

Finn inhaled deeply. He was rushing them because he wanted time with Ivy, but they'd had a long day. Lina had kept them extra, until halfway through the opening, and then they'd barely seen their mom at the café. Surely he could scrounge up some patience.

"How 'bout I brush them for you this time?" Sage showed slight interest at that. "We've got to get the sugar bugs out of your teeth. They might be multiplying right now."

She giggled and came his way slowly.

"Open up. Let me see."

She opened wide, and he mock-yelled, "Oh, no! There's so many of them. We have to catch them!"

Sage laughed and squealed. When he put toothpaste on her toothbrush, she let him check all over her mouth for the pesky invisible offenders. By the time he was done with her, Lola and Reese were lined up for the same, even though they'd already brushed.

Finn took his time, making them giggle, enjoying them again now that he'd stopped focusing on himself.

Just as he finished with their teeth, the front door opened, and Ivy came in. The girls rushed her, and she knelt to scoop them all into a hug.

"Best part of my day."

"They're ready for bed. Teeth are brushed."

"Mista Finn found sugar bugs in our teeth, Mommy." Sage relayed the information with a serious tone. "But he gotted them all."

"It's true. I did. I'm a master sugar bug tracker and destroyer."

Ivy's mouth twisted as she studied him, confusion wrinkling her forehead. What was that about?

"Let's get you girls into bed. It's late, and tomorrow's another early day."

"Nervous about the official opening?" Finn asked.

"Something like that. Can you stay for a minute while I tuck them in? I need to talk to you."

"Sure." Could it be so easy? He'd been wondering how to manage what she'd just asked of him without overstaying his welcome.

Ivy was in the girls' room for about two minutes. In that time, Finn paced and then sat, then got up to pace again.

When she came out, she looked worn and tired, and by instinct, he walked in her direction, opened his arms and pulled her close.

She stiffened and then released a wounded exhale as she relaxed against his chest.

"Long day?"

She nodded but didn't speak. They stayed that way for a time, his hope buoying. All he wanted was this on repeat. This and the chance to love her.

Ivy's shoulders straightened as if she'd heard his thoughts and disagreed with them. She backed out of his embrace, and his lonely arms fell to his sides.

"I shouldn't have let myself go there with you just now, but somehow you lure me in."

"Lure?" That was a strong word for a hug.

"Yes, *lure*." She began pacing the length of the short space, unknowingly following the path he'd just been on. "You confuse me so much. One minute you're a jerk." Ouch. He had fought hard to distance himself from her in the beginning. "And then you turn into my friend…and my rock." His mouth dried as her eyes shimmered with moisture. "And then I find out who you really are."

"What do you mean who I really am?" A dull throbbing began to beat inside his skull. This conversation wasn't going in the direction he'd hoped it would.

"When you brought up the stuff with the woman in North Dakota, I thought she'd just hurt you. And you let me believe that."

His gut crashed to the ground.

"But tonight, when I was talking to Charlie, I found out the rest of the story." Her finger jutted in his direction. "And don't you dare blame your sister. I told her I knew what had happened with you and this other woman in North Dakota, because I believed you'd told me all of it. I didn't have any reason to assume you hadn't."

Finn's tongue was a boulder—useless and heavy.

Ivy stopped directly across from him. "We stood right here and almost kissed. And you implied that you couldn't get involved with me because of the past—because of being hurt. But you hid your real reason to avoid anything with me." Finn's lids shuttered because he couldn't handle the stark pain claiming her pretty features. "I was a mess. My life is a mess. And you were trying not to get involved with another woman like the one in North Dakota."

He met her gaze, willing her to see everything he felt. "You are nothing like her."

"No? You didn't see a woman who needed rescuing when you rolled up on the girls and me after we slid off the road?" The noise she made was somewhere between a snort and a cry. "And the worst part is, I'm so mortified that you thought of me like that and I didn't have a clue. Once you started changing and opening up, I kept wondering if you could be real. If a man like you actually existed, or if my instincts were dead wrong once again."

His hands snaked out to grasp her arms. "Ivy, I exist. I'm the good version, not the bad. I promise."

Her head tilted in her listening position as if asking him to prove it. "Did you or did you not avoid a relationship or any romantic feelings for me because of how my life is in turmoil? And because you didn't want to get involved with another woman who was like the last one? Admit it. When you saw me, you saw a huge mess. Admit it!"

Finn had never witnessed this side of Ivy. She'd taken him to task after their almost kiss, but that had been nothing compared to the sea she currently resembled, the waves crashing and angry and hurting.

The itch to bury his initial reaction and fears over her was so strong that Finn's knees wobbled like a bowl of Jell-O in a toddler's hands. But not leveling with her now wouldn't help anything. They couldn't build a relationship on that. But once he admitted it, there wouldn't be anything to build.

"I don't think that way now."

"But you did in the beginning."

Finn let the silence answer since he couldn't bring himself to. "I was wrong. Now I know you. I was still recovering from Chrissa, and I let that fear win. I can see now that you're not that person. You're so strong, Ivy. So amazing. And I—"

"Stop." Her hand came up. "You didn't listen to me once. We were standing right here." She pointed to their feet. "And now it's my turn." Her eyes flitted to the door. They no longer held the hint of moisture. Instead they were fierce with resolve. "Go. Leave. Get out. Please."

It was the please that slayed him. The broken notes in it. The harm he'd done. If she wasn't willing to listen, how could Finn convince her that he'd been an idiot? That he'd figured out that she didn't need rescuing. No, that was him. He was the mess, not her.

So he did what she asked. He left even though every part of him wanted to stay and fight for her. She'd made her decision, and he had no choice but to respect it.

Chapter Fifteen

On Tuesday morning, Finn rose early for Bible study. A peek through the blinds told him Ivy's Suburban was still at the bunkhouse. His muscles unwound. Every day that Ivy and the girls remained was a victory. Part of the reason he'd obeyed her orders to *get out* and then continued to leave her alone was so that she and the girls wouldn't become flight risks.

He'd managed to go five days without seeing or pressuring Ivy. Five days of missing her. Five days of not sleeping. Five days of kicking himself for ruining them before they'd even had a chance.

He had not, on the other hand, managed to leave his sister alone for that long. When he'd had lunch with Charlie and Ryker after church on Sunday, he'd begged her to tell him if Ivy was planning to stay in Westbend or planning to move to California. She'd refused to give him any details.

Ivy specifically asked me not to talk to you about her. And to stay out of things between you both. I respect Ivy too much to break that promise, even for you.

Anger and frustration had formed a ball in his stomach. And yet, none of this was Charlie's fault. Nope. That blame was all on him.

Finn arrived at church ten minutes before the study started. He grabbed coffee and a pastry and sat at the oblong table. A minute later, Ryker took the seat next to him. He squeezed Finn's shoulder as if to say *I'm here and I'm sorry.*

"Any new developments?"

"No. She didn't come running over yesterday to tell me she forgives me and she's crazy in love with me." His voice cracked with the finesse of a teenager.

"Woman problems?" Jace Hawke questioned as he passed behind Finn. "We've all been there."

"Amen," Evan commented as he took the seat next to Finn, Jace sitting to his left.

"Speak for yourself," Jacob Blair retorted from across the table. "I met Jenny when we were in college and it was easy as can be. Never had a question or a doubt. We didn't fight. We just knew."

The table was full now with most of the men who attended study, and many of them exchanged winces at Jacob's proclamation.

"I think you're the exception to the rule, Jacob." Luc Wilder set his Bible and a notebook on the table. "So, Finn, what's the issue? Might as well lay it out now that we're all involved."

Finn crossed his arms. "We are not dissecting my issues as a group."

"But we have time before we start." Luc's hands spread wide, as if that was reason enough for Finn to air his dirty laundry.

When he didn't fill in, Ryker—the traitor—spoke for him. "He and Ivy Darling had a falling-out of sorts."

"Of sorts." Finn snorted and narrowed his eyes at Ryker. "Thanks for spilling the tea."

Ryker shrugged in innocence. "What? No one was going to let it go."

"Well?" Luc asked. "Did you commit the crime she's accusing you of?"

The chances of him getting out of this discussion now that it had begun were slim.

"I like how you just assume it's my fault…but, yes. I get why she's upset with me." Yes, Finn had avoided falling for Ivy because he'd assumed her life was a mess. But that was before he knew her. Now he saw all of her. And the struggles she'd been through were part of what made her so attractive to him. Neither of them was perfect by any means, but he was no longer afraid she needed rescuing. She'd saved him, not the other way around. How could she not see that? Because he hadn't told her, and now she wouldn't listen. His fear had kept him from her, and now it was ruining everything. What if she didn't give him another chance? How could he make her listen?

"Then there's only one thing to do." Luc steepled his fingers. "You have to fight for her."

Gage Frasier, who'd obviously been listening while filling his coffee cup, took a seat next to Luc. "Does she know how you feel? Because that can get you in a lot of trouble if you've been trying to hide it and she doesn't." He cleared amusement from his throat. "Not that I know that from experience or anything."

Jace leaned around Evan. "You should just march over there, confess you're crazy about her, and then throw her over your shoulder and elope. It's the best way."

The thought of throwing Ivy over his shoulder and forcing her to listen had its appeal, but Finn wasn't sure how well that would go. He pictured Ivy taking him to task much like she had in the café or at the bunkhouse. She could be feisty when the situation called for it. And eloping was definitely out of the question.

"I don't think that's going to work. We haven't known each other for years like you did Mackenzie."

Jace nodded contemplatively. "Yeah, I guess that's true."

"I'm sure she's hurt because you didn't tell her your initial thoughts," Evan chimed in.

Finn was very much starting to regret his decision to text with Ryker and Evan regarding Ivy over the last few days. They were certainly willing to assist in this public exposure of his distress.

"But how could I tell her my initial thoughts? They were terrible. They're the reason she's so hurt."

"It makes sense that you didn't," Evan responded. "But now that she found them out, you have to convince her how you feel *now*."

"There's really nothing to do but tell her you love her and force her to listen." Ryker added his two cents' worth. "Then she'll say her piece, and you can accept it. But trying to figure things out by yourself, in your own head, without her input…it's not going to work. You have to go to the source." He gave a rough sigh. "Sometimes our internal stuff has such a tight hold on us that we forget that God's wiped it all clean. That the past doesn't own us."

Finn had definitely let the past own him for too long. He'd been trying to move beyond the Chrissa failure and now the mess with Ivy on his own. With his own strength. But he could see that he wasn't enough. Only God was.

"All right, all right. Let's get to the actual study. You chicks can discuss my lack of a love life more later."

A round of laughter ended the conversation. The subject of Ivy didn't come up again until the end of study, when prayer requests were being mentioned.

"Put Finn on the list." Jace pointed to the sheet that held their prayer requests. "He's going to need it."

Laughter echoed again.

"Should really put down Ivy. She might need it more." That jab came from Evan.

"I thought you guys were supposed to be on my side."

"We are." Ryker slapped him on the back. "We're praying for your sorry hide, aren't we?"

Finn chuckled despite the painful truth of it. Their ribbing was simply that, and he would do the same to any of them if they were in his boots. Funny. He'd gone from not sharing anything when he'd left North Dakota to being okay with the whole men's Bible study knowing his problems. Wouldn't Charlie be proud of him for opening up now.

They bowed their heads to pray for each other, and Finn found his mind could only concentrate on prayers over the situation with Ivy. He'd make up the other prayers later, once his mind calmed and he could think straight again.

Lord, will You show me a way out of this mess I created? Help me to love Ivy well, whatever that looks like and wherever she and the girls end up.

Amen.

"You feeling okay, Kaia?"

The younger woman seemed distracted this morning, and Ivy was desperate to focus on someone besides herself and her problems.

Kaia glanced up from the table she was wiping. "What? Oh, I'm fine. Just overthinking."

"Overthinking what? I'm an expert on that subject. Maybe I can help."

"I had coffee with Maxwell last night." Ah. *Maxwell*, not Max. "He asked if we could be friends right now. He said he's interested in me but understands where I'm coming from."

"And? What are you thinking?"

"I don't know." Kaia returned the milk to the cooler, distractedly leaving the door ajar. Ivy covertly closed it after she'd walked away. "I mean, he's really great, but I should be concentrating on Honor right now. But having someone to talk to…that was pretty amazing. Having a friend like Maxwell could make me a better mom because it would be a step toward taking care of myself. My counselor says I need to do that. So which is the right answer? What's best for Honor? Or for me? And are those things the same or different?"

Ivy's jaw had unhinged with each declaration and question from Kaia. She felt the other woman's confusion in the marrow of her bones. Kaia had just stated exactly what Ivy had gone through when she'd been forced to make a decision for her and the girls. What was best? Colorado or California? And who was it best for? Ivy had finally concluded that giving her girls the best life didn't mean living with her parents, where everything was at their fingertips. She'd finally concluded that the girls seeing her work hard and save and budget would be better for them than not ever having a financial worry. She'd chosen the scarier route, because she believed it was the right one for all of them. And then if things changed or it didn't work, she'd readjust. Who said every decision had to be perfect the first time?

"Everything you said makes so much sense. I was just there. I still am there." Each day Ivy woke up wondering if she'd made the right choice. And then each day she shoved that doubt aside and took one tentative step after another. "A friend isn't a bad thing, Kaia. It could be really good for you to have someone to talk to. And if Max is that patient…that says a lot about who he is."

"Thank you." Kaia didn't often show physical affection, so her impromptu hug surprised Ivy. "I needed that release."

She squeezed the other woman. "Be kind to yourself, Kaia. Don't spend the next years cowering and beating yourself up. I speak from experience when I say it's not worth it."

Kaia's eyes were dark and glimmering as she eased back. "I'm working on it."

"And remember, sometimes the right man can come along at the wrong time. So maybe in the future…"

Kaia laughed and turned to help a new customer.

Ivy firmly believed that Kaia could have both a healthy romantic relationship and a healthy mother-daughter relationship raising Honor, but she'd have to come to those terms on her own.

Which means I could have the same with my three girls and the right man.

Ivy had just begun to consider that when everything had imploded with Finn. Now it was her and her girls indefinitely…and she would be okay with that. Somehow.

The morning after their argument, Ivy had expected

Finn to show up at her door with another explanation or apology. But she hadn't seen him since the night of the café opening.

And now that she wouldn't be living on his land anymore, the likelihood that they would cross paths soon was diminishing.

At least she had plenty to keep her occupied with packing up the bunkhouse. Ivy was amazed by how fast their few belongings had multiplied into such a mess.

Mess. She rolled her eyes at the word she now hated. The one that Finn believed represented her. Ivy wished they had never met. That he could never have formed such an opinion about her.

No, you don't. He has your heart. That's what makes this all hurt so badly.

Ivy ignored the pang of awareness. For all of her work in recognizing her feelings and letting herself feel all the things since Lee's death, she'd taken the opposite fork in the road regarding what had happened with Finn.

She'd stopped processing it. Stopped thinking about it and him. *Like right now?*

Thankfully, the café experienced a rush during lunch that carried into the afternoon, and Ivy was able to pour herself into work.

Just before she planned to lock up and leave to pick up the triplets, Charlie stopped by. Kaia had taken the early shift this morning, so she'd already left for the day.

"How's it going?" Charlie's attempt to be casual failed miserably and left no doubt as to her actual thoughts: *Are you okay? Do I need to beat up my brother? I'm trying not to get involved even though I've never wanted anything more.*

"Has anyone ever told you that you're terrible at hiding what you're thinking?"

Charlie chuckled. "I may have heard that a time or two. I don't— I just—" Her palms went up. "Never mind. I'm staying out of it like you asked me to, so… Moving on… How's the packing going?"

"I did a little last night. We don't have much, but it's still a lot to sort through. I should be able to wrap up tonight as long as the girls aren't a hindrance." Ivy winced, imagining just how rambunctious the three of them would likely be. With yet another move and change on the horizon, they'd been acting cranky and out of sorts.

Just like their mom.

The triplets asked her numerous times a day where Mista Finn was and why they hadn't seen him in weeks and weeks. Their concept of time was terrible, but the distance had felt just as long to Ivy, so she couldn't blame their interpretation of the situation.

"Let me take them for a bit. Give you some time to organize without them underfoot."

"Oh, no. I can't do that. We'll be fine, Charlie. Besides, I have to get used to doing things on my own with them now that I've committed to staying."

When Ivy had told her parents that she and the girls had found a small house to rent and were planning to stay in Westbend, they'd responded with anger and confusion. She'd talked to them for almost an hour before getting anywhere. And the only way she'd made headway was to ask them to come visit. She wanted them to see the town and the café and the new life she and the girls had begun, because maybe then they would understand her choice.

Ivy had asked them for the grace to make a mistake by staying.

They'd called her back the next day, and in a completely unexpected olive branch, had offered to ship her and the girls' things to Colorado.

Ivy had wept with relief and gratefulness. She didn't want to lose her parents over her choice, but she also didn't want to lose herself. And that had been the thought that had scared her the most about continuing on to California. She'd grown in Westbend, and she couldn't leave that confidence behind. Though it had been chopped down by Finn, she was determined to build it back up again. It was time to stand on her own two feet...while holding on to God with a tight grip, of course.

Charlie's hand squeezed hers. "I'm not asking. I'm telling you. I would love to have the girls for a bit. It's a nice day. I'll take them to the park and wear them out. Can you let Lina know I'm picking them up and shoot me her address?"

"Okay." It was no use fighting Charlie. She'd get her way, and Ivy was grateful for her stubbornness right now. "Thank you."

"Of course. I'll text you when I'm bringing them home."

Ivy arrived at the ranch determined to pack quickly while she had time to herself. The small two-bedroom house she'd rented in town was furnished and currently unoccupied, so they could move in anytime. Tomorrow would be ideal, as she hoped to remove herself and the girls from Finn's ranch as quickly as possible.

She folded and boxed clothes with worship music blaring, separating out what would need to be washed at the new place. It had a washer and dryer, so Ivy would be able to do laundry easily…without using Finn's facilities.

I am not going to miss him. I am not even going to think about him.

After making numerous trips to the Suburban—and not allowing herself one peek toward Finn's house—she started on her own clothes.

A knock sounded on her door, and Ivy's heart pounded in answer. Would Charlie be back with the girls already?

Highly unlikely.

She swung it open to see Finn's tall, broad frame filling the space, his sad, soulful eyes no doubt matching her current condition.

"I thought I saw you packing your vehicle."

"I am."

His lids shuttered. "Oh." The breath visibly leaked from his chest like he was a balloon with a pin prick.

"What do you want, Finn?"

"You." Her stomach bottomed out. "And the girls. I miss you."

I miss you, too. Her soul tapped out the admission like Morse code, and she was ever so thankful she hadn't said it out loud.

"Are the girls home?" He peered around her and into the bunkhouse. She was tempted to tell him they were, but the lack of noise and chaos would clue him in that they weren't.

"Charlie took them for a bit after work so I could pack."

"Ivy." His voice cracked on her name, and her heart followed suit. "Will you please listen to me for a minute? I have to tell you what happened." Despite asking, he didn't wait for her answer. He just roared on with his speech. "You were right—I did judge your situation and your story when I first met you. But I was an idiot, and I figured that out pretty quickly. I'm sorry for assuming your life was chaos and that I shouldn't get involved. Chrissa did mess with me, but you're not her. You're nothing like her. She always took, but you've *never* been that way. You always gave. The issues were all mine, not yours. And now I'm afraid… I can't believe I'm going to lose you." The words were muffled as he rubbed his hands over his face.

Going to? Hadn't he already lost her? And could you call it losing someone when you'd never crossed the start line?

"If I knew you were moving because it was the best decision for you and the girls, I'd figure out how to let you go. Somehow. But the thought that your leaving might have something to do with me and my stupid mistakes… I don't know how to handle that."

His head hung low.

He thought she was moving to California. Charlie hadn't told her brother they were staying in town. Ivy had asked her to stay out of it, but she hadn't expected that kind of loyalty. It only cemented her decision to stay. Ivy had chosen to live in Westbend because it was where she wanted to raise her girls. Not solely because she was in love with Finn Brightwood. But now she was starting to fear he might have a little something to do with the decision.

"Every compliment you gave me…was it all lies?" He'd told her he respected her and was impressed with how she handled the girls. That she was doing a good job as a mom. And yet…how could she now believe anything he'd said?

"None of it was lies. All of those things are true about you. I just let that initial fear from what had happened with Chrissa cloud my judgment."

Her nerves were as skittish as Reese in a new social situation, and tears pooled along her lower lids. "What if I'm a mess again, Finn? Right now or in ten years? I can't be with someone who wouldn't love me through that. I can't be with someone who runs at the first sign of trouble." It scared her so much to imagine trusting Finn now…only to find out later she'd been wrong. Again.

"Ivy." His hands grasped her arms, then slid down to her wrists, his thumbs skidding across her thundering pulse. "You are not a mess. And even if you were, that would be fine, too. All I know is that I want you exactly as you are. You're a fighter. You're lightning and rain and sunshine all wrapped into one. I don't know how to go a day without you." Watery emotion weighted down his words, causing an echo in her soul. "I want to be with you. I want to come home to you and have dinner with you and the girls and talk about our days and pray together. I want to carry the girls to bed when they're sleepy and tuck them in. I want to know everything about you and find out how to love you best." Tears blurred her vision. "My first impression changed quickly because I saw who you really are. Can you see who I really am? Can you see me beyond a stupid choice or opinion?"

Could she? Could she believe in Finn? In both of them? And in her God-given intuition?

"I promised myself that I'd stay out of your decision to stay or go. That I wouldn't try to control you like Lee.

That's why I didn't say anything earlier, when I first began falling for you. I didn't want to affect your choice in any way. And now it doesn't matter, because you've already made up your mind. And as long as you're happy, then I'll find a way to be that for you. Because I trust you to make good decisions, Ivy. Don't doubt your instincts. They're still good. They're still right."

Ivy had been afraid that she'd missed the signs with Finn the same way she'd missed them with Lee. But in this moment, clarification struck. She hadn't missed any red flags with Finn, because they didn't exist. How could she have ever thought this man wasn't good to the very last drop?

"Finn, we're not moving to California." She held her breath as understanding struck him.

"You're staying?"

She began to nod, but before she could complete the movement, his lips were on hers, and she was otherwise occupied. Kissing Finn was like coming home. Like careening off the road and finding out where you were meant to be all along.

He rested his forehead against hers, his gentle palms cradling her face. "Please give me a chance to prove how I feel about you and that it's never going to change. Give me a chance to love you and the girls. Let me show you who I am."

Ivy wanted nothing more than to move forward with Finn in their lives. Her hands slipped up to cover his. "I know who you are."

That earned her another kiss. It was slow and sweet, and her knees swirled like creamer melting into hot coffee.

Finn reared back as if a bee had crawled under his

shirt and was waging war against his skin. "Wait. So where are you moving, then?"

"Just into town."

He frowned. "You don't have to go. You can stay here."

"We can't, though. It's time for us to have our own place. I suppose I have a few things to prove yet—that I can take care of the girls and make it on our own. Without handouts."

His mouth curved reluctantly. "Well, don't take too long."

Her smile mimicked his. She didn't plan to.

"How'd the conversation that you're staying go with your parents?"

"About like you'd expect at first, but I invited them to come visit, and I'm hoping once they see us here, they'll understand. And if they don't… I still believe this was the right decision for me and the girls."

He squeezed her hand. "I'm proud of you for trusting your instincts."

"Thank you." She laced her fingers through his, reveling in Finn's confidence in her. "So will you be meeting them as my special friend or my former hesitant landlord?" Finn had told her about his parents' amusing label for anyone he'd dated.

"Special friend, for sure." His eyes danced with humor, then turned earnest. "If you're willing to give me a chance, Ivy Darling, I'm not going to let you go. I'm in this—with you *and* the girls—for the long haul."

The way he always included the girls liquefied her. Ivy had tried with all her strength not to fall swiftly for Finn because she'd believed it would end in disaster. But then he'd gone and loved her girls swiftly, and that had been the tipping point in her descent. Turned out falling fast and furiously wasn't detrimental when the man on the other end of her adoration was wholesome and good and Finn Brightwood.

She could choose Finn just for the way he championed her girls, but loving him—finally letting herself feel all she did—was selfishly for her.

Her heart thrashed against her ribs as Finn's fingers threaded through her hair and his lips found hers again, this kiss less urgent but just as tender. As if they had all the time in the world to get to know each other, love each other, grow old together.

He delivered a kiss to the corner of her mouth, then he traveled to the other side to do the same, making her skin tingle with expectation. Warmth enveloped her, and when he scooped her into his arms and held her so tight she could barely breathe, Ivy knew without a doubt that this town and this man were where she and the girls were supposed to land.

Just like God had known all along.

Epilogue

The grass surrounding the ranch house was full of children and adults mingling under the warm October sun. Ivy had prepped for Charlie and Ryker's adoption shower as much as she could beforehand, but she was still running.

Finn must have spotted her rushing from across the yard because he followed her into the kitchen.

"What do you need me to do?"

"Grab the pickles. And those jars with the candy. I should have set those out before since they're part of the decorations, but I didn't want the kids getting into them early."

Finn gathered the items she'd mentioned while Ivy took the fixings for grilled burgers from the fridge. When she turned, Finn had set the items back on the counter. He took the serving plates from her and did the same, and then his arms came around her. Well, as much as they could when her pregnant belly extended between them.

"I just need to hold you for a second." The girls' saying gained a smile, and she relaxed against her husband. She could stop rushing. No one would know she had a schedule written out for what food should be served when. No one would know she'd stolen thirty seconds in the kitchen with the man she loved.

In two short months, they would celebrate their two-year wedding anniversary. Almost two years of choosing to love each other, choosing to communicate, choosing to laugh. Finn had become a father to the girls. They called him Dad or Daddio or Pops—whatever fit their fancy each day—and he beamed every single time.

His kiss pressed against her hair. "You feeling okay?"

"I feel great." Except for the intermittent Braxton-Hicks contractions that had plagued her since this morning. But there was no reason to concern Finn. They were common a few weeks out.

The pregnancy had been a surprise. Ivy hadn't known if she'd be able to get pregnant, and so they'd decided they'd be fine either way. They had the girls, and they were enough. But their little boy, who was due in thirteen days, would be a welcome addition to the family.

When Ivy made a move to leave Finn's arms, he tugged her back against him. "I'm not done yet."

She laughed, her voice muffled against his shirt. "Your sister is going to think I've forgotten this shower is about her."

"Charlie and Ryker are having a great time. They're not going to notice a thing."

The celebrating parents had married three months after the opening of the café. The next year, they'd begun fostering a three-year-old and his baby sister. Today was the celebration of their adoption.

Ivy inhaled the scent of Finn, letting it flow down to ease her aching back and legs. "Okay, now we really do need to get out there."

Finn released her. "Yes, ma'am." They each grabbed the items they'd been holding and headed back into the sunshine. "Who would have thought this many families could produce this many children?"

Their family had become friends with many of the families of the men who attended Bible study with Finn.

When Ivy and the girls had slid off the road, never could she have imagined all of this would be waiting for her. Not only had she gained a husband who was her best friend, her girls had gained an amazing father, and she'd also built friendships that she couldn't fathom finding anywhere else. Deep and true and abiding. Community was a beautiful thing, and Ivy hadn't realized how much she'd been missing it until she'd happened upon it in Westbend.

And to think she and the girls had come so close to leaving Colorado after her falling-out with Finn. It was only by the grace of God that they'd stayed, and He'd healed all of them in so many ways.

Finn set the food items on the table and went to start the grill.

"Do you need any help with that?" Emma Frasier, who was married to Gage, approached just as Ivy dropped off her items and began organizing.

"You're sweet to offer, but we can handle it." Ivy was hosting with Addie, who had just waved and walked in the direction of the house, which meant she was grabbing the other sides. "You just relax." Emma was carting around her seven-month-old—little Zeke—but it wasn't in her nature *not* to offer to assist.

Her older son was running around with the big kids, who were playing tag. Jace and Mackenzie's son, fittingly named Wilder after his mom's maiden name and perfectly representing his personality, took a tumble in the dirt but quickly righted himself so as to avoid missing out.

"I otay!" He popped up and rejoined the game, causing the adults to laugh.

Addie arrived with the sides and set them on the table, adding serving spoons. She'd put Evan on baby duty today, which meant he was currently chasing their little one-year-old girl as she attempted to chase her big brother.

A car pulled into the ranch drive, and Addie shaded her eyes. "Who's that?"

"Kaia and Max," Ivy answered. "He told me the other day he's been shopping for engagement rings. The two of them sure took their sweet time getting to this point. Probably not a bad thing with all Kaia and Honor have been through."

Honor jumped out of the back seat of the car and ran to catch up with the kids, midgame. Kaia waved in Ivy's direction as they exited the vehicle, and then she and Max joined some other young couples from church, their linked hands making Ivy smile.

Oh. Ivy placed a hand on her lower back and stopped to breathe deeply through the pain.

"You okay?" Addie questioned, studying her.

"I'm fine. Just having a few Braxton-Hicks contractions."

Charlie joined them, obviously overhearing the end of their conversation. "Really? How often?"

"This morning not as much, but now they're happening more regularly."

Like moths to a flame, Mackenzie Hawke and Cate Wilder, Luc's wife, also joined the conversation. "What's happening over here? Do you all need help with anything?"

"Ivy's having contractions but thinks they're only Braxton-Hicks." At Addie's declaration, Ivy's lids shuttered.

"Addie," she scolded the woman. No need to broadcast it to the whole group.

"What? It's true. But I'm not sure you're not having actual contractions."

"Let's get you a chair." Emma found a lawn chair and brought it to Ivy. "Just sit a minute. Maybe you've been doing too much."

"I told you hosting right now wasn't a good idea." Charlie's arms crossed, her concern evident.

Hands on Ivy's shoulders gently pushed her into the chair.

"I'm fine. You're all overreacting."

"Did you go into labor with the girls?" Emma asked.

"No. I had a cesarean."

"And you said you've been feeling these all day?" Mackenzie questioned.

"Yes, but they're not terrible."

"Hmm." Mackenzie frowned. "I didn't have terrible contractions before having Wilder." As if in answer, her son gave a whoop and pretended to strike down a cousin with a fake sword. She laughed at the play. "Like mother, like son. I'm just going to grab Jace. He's trained in these things as an EMT."

"Wait! I promise I'm…fine."

Mackenzie either didn't hear or she wasn't listening. She returned in a moment with Jace in tow. Finn followed Jace, as had the other men he'd been talking to near the grill, which meant now Ivy was sitting in a lawn chair in the middle of a crowd, completely on display, completely embarrassed. Finn rounded the group to stand next to her. He slid a hand under her hair and massaged the back of her neck.

Oh, that felt good.

Jace began asking her numerous questions that he obviously used in his work.

"When did the pain start?"

"This morning." She'd woken to them, actually, attributing it to excitement over today.

"Are the contractions in your abdomen? Or your back or where?"

"Kind of everywhere, I guess. Lower back is where they started, though now I'm feeling it more..." She motioned to her abdomen and legs, because yeah, the last hour or so, it had been traveling.

"You need to go in, Ivy. I think you're in labor."

"When I had the twins, if I hadn't gone in when I did..." Cate Wilder fought back emotion. "It's not worth risking anything. It's always best to get checked." Luc tucked his wife against his side, comforting her. Ivy had heard their story, but the twins had come very early and Cate had suffered health complications. Their situations were different.

Ivy's sigh was audible. But Cate—and everyone—was right. It wasn't worth the risk.

"Fine. I'll go in." The table full of gifts sat to her left, so full, so pretty. "But I'm hosting a shower." Her declaration ended with a moan. She'd been looking forward to this shower for over a month.

"Cohosting," Addie chimed in. "I can handle the hosting, or we can postpone until we know more."

"Wait? What? No way. If I'm being forced to go to the hospital, even though these are false contractions, then you all are going to continue this shower. It's happening." Ivy stared down every last one of them. "Got it?"

She was answered with a chorus of *Yes, ma'am*s.

Once she and Finn were assured that their guests would continue the party—and take care of the triplets—they grabbed the birthing bag and drove to the hospital.

Two short hours later, Ivy held their beautiful, healthy newborn son in her arms.

Finn settled on the edge of the bed as the nurses and doctor gave them a minute alone with their latest addition.

"If we hadn't left when we did, you might have had our son on the side of the road." Finn's amused grin still had the power to make her stomach do cartwheels. "Fitting for how I first met you."

Ivy groaned. "That would have been terrible." She ran her fingers over the baby's incredibly soft cheeks. "But we would have survived it."

"We would have. Like we do anything—together." Finn kissed her forehead, lingering, tender. "You were amazing, Ivy. I've never seen you stronger."

"Must be some sort of natural instinct that kicks in." She traced the baby's tiny fingers, marveling at the miniature nails. "What are you thinking about for a name?"

They had a list and some top contenders, but they'd wanted to wait to meet him before deciding for certain.

Finn studied the baby, pride and joy evident. "Let's say which name we like best at the same time."

"Okay. One, two, three…"

"Marshall."

They both said Finn's grandfather's name—which was also his middle name. The family patriarch had passed away peacefully in his sleep about a year ago, but the impact he'd had on his children and grandchildren and great-grandchildren would never be forgotten.

"Perfect name." Ivy lifted her chin for a kiss, and Finn bent, his lips warm and comforting on hers.

"Perfect baby." Finn shifted more onto the bed with her, propping his long legs down the mattress and tucking his arm around her back. He touched the baby's nose and earned a wrinkled brow in response, making them both laugh. "Welcome to the world, little Marshall. You're already loved by so many."

It was true—both her parents and Finn's were more than ready to be involved in Marshall's life, just like both already doted on the girls. Each set of grandparents visited often, and things had smoothed considerably between Ivy and her parents as they'd witnessed her growing ability to stand up for herself and make wise decisions…including the one to love and choose the man currently holding her.

"Your sisters are going to flip out when they see you. Do the girls know yet?" Ivy checked with Finn.

"No. Charlie and Ryker took them back to their place after the shower wrapped up, but she's not going to tell them until we give her the go-ahead. She wondered if we'd want to have her bring them to the hospital so we can surprise them."

"Let's do it. They will lose their little minds with excitement."

"That they will. I keep thinking about how we wouldn't have any of this if you hadn't given me a second chance back when I botched things up. I'm glad you didn't give up on me, Ivy. On us."

Her eyes closed as the emotion of today wrapped around her like his warm hug. "I can't imagine life without you. I can't imagine even one day of not loving you back."

Most men would run away from rather than toward the kind of mess she'd been when arriving in Westbend. Ivy could look back now and see what Finn had first witnessed. She didn't blame him for his initial wariness of her. But she was eternally grateful they'd both moved past those preliminary reactions.

Her theory that Finn Brightwood was a generous, caring, beautiful soul and not the closed-off version of himself that he'd portrayed when they'd first met had been proven correct time and time again. He was perfect for her and the girls…and now Marshall.

"God bless you, Finn Brightwood."

His chest vibrated with a chuckle. "There is no *me* in this. Only us. So I think the phrase you're looking for is 'God bless *us*.'"

Ivy's smile bloomed as Finn stole Marshall from her, the baby somehow appearing even tinier in his strong hands. Her husband couldn't be more right.

* * * * *

If you've missed any of these romances in Jill Lynn's Colorado Grooms series, go back and pick them up!

The Rancher's Surprise Daughter *(Cate & Luc)*
The Rancher's Unexpected Baby *(Emma & Gage)*
The Bull Rider's Secret *(Mackenzie & Jace)*
Her Hidden Hope *(Addie & Evan)*
Raising Honor *(Charlie & Ryker)*

All available now from Love Inspired Books!

Dear Reader,

I can't believe this series has come to an end. It's hard for me to let go of these characters I've grown to love. Thank you for reading and celebrating each book with me. Without you, I wouldn't get to dream and make up stories, and for that I am so grateful. Throughout this series, there have been highs and lows, but God has been consistent every step of the way. He provided the words and the scenes, and I'm so grateful He carried these books through to completion.

My prayer for you (and me) is that we see God's hand in our lives—even in the unexpected. Ivy's journey was a complete surprise, and yet, she's exactly where she's supposed to be. May we all feel that peace and guidance in our own lives, too.

To keep up with book news or find my latest giveaway, head to Jill-Lynn.com/news. I'm also on Facebook.com/JillLynnAuthor and Instagram.com/JillLynn Author, and I would love to connect with you there.

Thank you for reading!
Jill Lynn

SPECIAL EXCERPT FROM

LOVE INSPIRED
INSPIRATIONAL ROMANCE

*Running a small Amish coffee shop is all Lydia Stoltzfus
needs to be satisfied with her life—until her next-door
neighbor and childhood crush, Simon Fisher, returns
home with his five-year-old daughter. Now, even as
she falls for the shy little girl, Lydia must resist her
growing feelings for Simon...*

Read on for a sneak preview of
A Secret Amish Crush *by Marta Perry.*
Available March 2021 from Love Inspired.

"You want me to say you were right about Aunt Bess
and the matchmaking, don't you? Okay, you were right,"
Simon said.

"I thought you'd come to see it my way," Lydia said
lightly. "It didn't take your aunt long to get started, did
it?"

His only answer was a growled one. "You wouldn't
understand."

"Look, I do see what the problem is," she said. "You
don't want people to start thinking that you're tied up
with me when you have someone else in mind."

"I don't have anyone in mind." Simon sounded as if
he'd reached the end of his limited patience. "I'm not
going to marry again—not you, not anyone. I found love
once, and I don't suppose anyone has a second chance at
a love like that."

LIEXP0221

His bleak expression wrenched her heart, and she couldn't find any response.

He frowned, staring at the table as if he were thinking of something. "What do you suppose would happen if I hinted to Aunt Bess that I was thinking that way, but that I really needed to get to know you without scaring you off?"

"I don't know. She might be even worse. Still, I guess you could try it."

"Not just me," he said. "You'd have to at least act as if you were willing to be friends."

Somehow she had the feeling that she'd end up regretting this. But on the other hand, he could hardly discourage her from trying to help Becky in that case.

"Just one thing. If we're supposed to be becoming friends, then you won't be angry if I take an interest in Becky now, will you?"

He nodded. "All right. But…" He seemed to grow more serious. "If this makes you uncomfortable for any reason, we stop."

She tried to chase away the little voice in her mind that said she'd get hurt if she got too close to him. "No problem," she said firmly, and slammed the door on her doubts.

Don't miss
A Secret Amish Crush
by Marta Perry, available wherever
Love Inspired books and ebooks are sold.

LoveInspired.com

LIEXP0221

LOVE INSPIRED

INSPIRATIONAL ROMANCE

UPLIFTING STORIES OF FAITH, FORGIVENESS AND HOPE.

Join our social communities to connect with other readers who share your love!

Sign up for the Love Inspired newsletter at **LoveInspired.com** to be the first to find out about upcoming titles, special promotions and exclusive content.

CONNECT WITH US AT:

Facebook.com/LoveInspiredBooks

Twitter.com/LoveInspiredBks

Facebook.com/groups/HarlequinConnection